I0620345

this can't be love

Leigh Verrill-Rhys

*What happens in Edinburgh stays in Edinburgh —
if Mike Argent has anything to say about it.*

this can't be love

by

Leigh Verrill-Rhys

An "Americans in Love" Novel

Published by Eres

Eres

EresBooks.com

ISBN 978-0-692361-900
ISBN 10: 0692361901

Cover Design: Gwion Dulais
Cover Photography: © Andreaobzerova | Dreamstime.com
Edinburgh Cityscape with Fireworks

dedication

for all the stand-up guys
and the dolls who find them

acknowledgments

encouragement comes in many guises and to those who
have offered enthusiasm, acknowledgement, cheers,
cups of coffee, red roses, chocolate and advice, thank
you.

one

"Did you see that?" Mike stamped the aggregate from the treads of his work boots. "What the hell?" His hard hat slammed into the barrier, his neck and shoulders rammed between the guardrail. Still on his feet, no bones broken, he ran straight at the roadster. Before he ripped the driver's door off its hinges, the passenger door walloped against the curb.

The roadster screamed away up Princes Street, its roar drowning the bagpipes and show hawkers only long enough for Mike to hear a sob.

One purple shoe tottered on the edge of the construction zone. The other clung to the twisted foot of a bare-legged girl.

Adrenaline pumped hard through his system, flashes of his collision with a fast car on an Arizona highway drove his temperature sky high. "Who was that jerk?"

The girl didn't hear him, too busy pulling the contents of her bag together, too busy pretending there was nothing strange about being shoved out of a car careening down an Edinburgh street where no cars were supposed to enter, too busy ignoring the stares of scores of tourists and the hulk of a construction worker standing over her.

"Are you all right?"

She didn't answer, just gave him one of those model's vacant stares, vaguely suggestive but too stupid to hold any lasting intrigue. Mike rolled his eyes and held out his hand to help her to her feet, wondering how anyone could walk on shoes with heels like needles.

She ignored his offer, pretended she didn't see his big fingers waggling under her chin.

A couple of his work crew came up behind him, asking questions, forming opinions, telling her story. Mike reached down to grasp her elbow. She yanked away to stand on her own. If he hadn't caught her, she'd have been in the pit.

She had the shortest hair of any girl he'd ever seen. "Whoa, now, lady. You've had a nasty shock."

"I'm fine," she huffed, pulling away and brushing her skirt. Short skirt. Nice legs. She bent to retrieve the shoe.

"Whoa, whoa, whoa," Mike said, holding her arm to keep her from toppling after her shoe. "One of you, go after that, will ya?"

Jimmy jumped down and held the shoe up. Mike plucked it from his foreman's hand. "Isn't going to be much good to you, lady. Heel's busted."

She pressed two fingers to her lips.

"Who was that jerk?"

"Boyfriend. Whatever," she said, holding out her hand, leaning hard on his arm. "Thanks." She ignored all the speculation hissing around them. "Thank you."

"Looks nasty."

"What? It's nothing."

"That cut. You'll need stitches."

She looked down at her arm, pinched together by his thick fingers but still bleeding. In a breath, she was limp, collapsing like a piece of string. All he could do was clasp her under her arms and stop her from ending up a ragged pile at his feet.

For a moment, the girl hung from his arms with his crew staring at him. And he stared down at her pure, pale face wondering what had happened. He hoisted her legs over his arm and stalked toward the site cabin, barking at his crew. The few tourists who had seen the incident lost interest in speculating.

Jimmy ran ahead and had the cabin door open when Mike got there.

"Ambulance, Mike?"

"Maybe." He cleaned most of the blood off her forearm so he could see the damage. "Where's the nearest ER?"

"ER?" Jimmy screwed up one side of face, deciphering. "Oh yeah. Casualty, right?"

"What else?"

"Come on, Mike, you've been here over a year and you still get pushed out of shape when we have a conflict of language."

Mike ignored the Scotsman and wrapped a first aid kit bandage around her arm. His patient should have been groaning in protest when she came round but her eyes roamed around the room for a moment before she looked at him.

"What happened?"

"You, uh, fell out of a car."

"What's this place?"

"Site office. On Princes Street. Do you remember anything?"

"I remember." She made a move to sit up, fell back against the arm of the grungy sofa. "Who are you?"

"Name's Mike. What's yours?"

"Jakki."

She wasn't communicative. He was curious. A pretty girl with nice legs didn't just fall out of a car every day. He'd used 'fell' to encourage her to talk. She wasn't talking. "You said the driver of that car was your boyfriend."

"Former boyfriend."

"I'm not surprised if he's been shoving you out of speeding cars for a while."

"What time is it,…Mike?" She wore a gargantuan watch but didn't bother to look at it.

"Three fifteen. How do you feel now?"

"A little shaky. I'll be all right," she said, comforting herself more than reassuring him.

Mike leaned forward to exam her arm for a moment. She turned her head away. Thinking the sight of blood made her sick, Mike checked the field dressing. Doing its job but she'd be better off with stitches, something better than a wad of gauze. "I'm taking you to the ER."

"Why?"

"You don't want to end up with an ugly scar, do you?"

"Will I?" She turned her arm to look at the bandage, lost color from her face in seconds and was almost comatose by the time he handed her a glass of water. "I don't like hospitals."

"Me either but they're a necessary evil in this case. Hold on while I get Jimmy to bring my truck around."

She looked at him as if he'd appeared from some other planet. "No thanks. I'll walk to the theater."

"What theater?"

"Where I work. I should be there."

"Lady, you're nuts. You're not going to any theater. You're staying where I can keep an eye on you or to the hospital. That's the deal. I'm calling the cops."

"What? Why?"

"You were shoved out of a car or don't you remember?"

Her face flamed. "I'm not stupid."

"Never said you were. But your ex-boyfriend has some explaining to do."

"You don't understand," Jakki said, pushing forward to sit up, dropping her feet to the cabin floor. "Where are my shoes?"

"Shoe. Right here." He held out the flimsy contraption. "The other one's broken."

"Do you know how much these cost?" She accused him. "Do you have any idea—."

"Listen, lady, I'm the good guy. You want to blame anyone, blame the jerk who dumped you in my construction site and sped off, right?"

"He wouldn't do that."

"No? Well that's just what he did and I'm taking you where you need to be. No argument." Alpha male in full flux. Did he ever learn?

6

"I have an appointment. This is The Fringe, you know."

"No kidding? Makes no difference to me, lady. You are in no condition—."

"I have to be at the theater in an hour."

"You're crazy. You can't even stand."

"I have to be there."

"What in hell is so important about that?"

"Obviously, you have never been called upon to perform professionally or otherwise." She reached to slide into her one shoe, dizziness sending her back against the sofa. "Limping along the street doesn't appeal to me right now, low on my list of accomplishments."

"At last, some sense."

"I have what it takes to be a professional." A whisper. A plea.

"Hey, I may be a Neanderthal, but you're in shock,… Jakki."

Another look like he was from another world, probably wondering how he knew her name. Standing on her own for her first feat of endurance, she was teetering on the heel from the moment she straightened her legs, wobbling on one bare foot. His told-you-so folded arms didn't offer any support when her backside landed on the sofa and she almost lost her lunch again.

"You don't understand. I have to go. I have to be there."

"Crazy. Listen, I'll take you if it's that important but first you're going to let me check you over."

"What do you mean?"

"Don't go getting all huffy and offended, dollface. I'm not just your ordinary Joe."

"I thought your name was Mark."

"Mike."

Her 'whatever' shrug went straight to the heart of the matter, like every man she'd ever met in her life claimed extraordinary individuality, hadn't met one yet who measured up to his own imagination. Mike smirked, sat on the edge of the table and pulled her arm straight out.

"You need stitches."

"No hospital. No doctor's office. No chance."

This girl was trouble, no doubt about that, but Mike had not found any reason for a jerk in a roadster to push her out of his car. He could think of a catalogue of reasons for pulling her in, starting with those long legs and not even close to ending with her buzzcut.

"You win, lady, but on one condition."

She looked at him as if she knew exactly what that condition was, had heard it all before and was utterly indifferent.

"That cut on your arm needs attention. Let me see to it and I won't insist on the hospital."

She eyed him now as if he were a creature from the swamp, the Neanderthal he admitted to; skepticism and suspicion battled it out for a few heartbeats before she shrugged and raised her arm for inspection. Mike peeled back the temporary dressing, frowned, turned her forearm this way and that. Still holding her wrist, he dragged the green first aid kit across the table and rummaged around.

"Are you staying nearby?"

"Not far," she replied, concentrating on the wall calendar.

Mike tore the packaging with his teeth and worked the butterfly bandages free with one hand. Her chin jutted upward but she never took her eyes off the photo of the girl advertising hardware, wearing a pouty look and not much else. A construction site guy thing, but Mike swallowed hard on what this girl might be thinking about him with barely-dressed women hanging over his desk. He lined the bandages up in the order he intended to apply them before he cleaned the wound of asphalt and grit.

"This will sting a bit."

She shrugged and braced herself.

"It will be easier if you relax, Jakki."

"That's what everyone says, just before they put an electrode in your brain."

Mike lifted his head just in time to see a tear catch on her lower lash and just as suddenly retract. "Did I hurt you?"

"No more than anyone else."

"I didn't mean to," he said, securing the end of the last butterfly bandage and inspecting his work. He searched her eyes for a moment, but there was no trace of the doleful regret he'd caught before, just a model's vacant stare, vaguely suggestive but too empty to be of interest for long. Somehow, that look didn't come naturally to this girl. Somehow, she had to work hard to look too stupid to grasp two-plus-two. "Are you hungry?"

"I never eat before a performance."

"What do you do?"

"Shop."

His grin was genuine and came seconds before a chuckle. Jimmy barged in again followed by a man in what looked like pajamas.

"This lad's a doctor, Mike."

His patient's whole body coiled without moving the smallest ligament. The vacant stare went to panic. "We're done, Doc. Thanks, but—."

"I'll just check her over. This man said she fell from a car. Could have concussion—."

Jakki rocketed out of the intern's reach and put Mike upfront, face to face with medical authority not to be denied. Her blind resistance, terror, her body smacked up against his back and she was close to losing consciousness. Whatever the girl felt, he couldn't let her faint then. He half-turned and slid his arm around her. "Sorry, mate. Miss Jackson is particular about her medical practitioners. Only goes private. Her physician's on the way. Spoke to him myself just now."

"I see," the intern said. "Sorry I bothered."

"Don't be, mate," Mike said tightening his arm a bit when *Miss Jackson* went a little too loose and dropped her head on his shoulder. "She's okay. Just a little shook up."

"I suppose you know how to treat shock," the doctor said more as a sneer than a question.

"A couple years of training helps," Mike said, taking most of her weight, what there was of it, on his hip. Vacant stares, weightless, long, tall, pale. *What had he gotten himself into?*

The intern shoved through the cabin door, rubbing his shoulder as he hopped down the steps and was gone in the crowds. No good. Mike let the girl down easy into a chair but she wasn't out. Dazed maybe. "Okay, sweetheart, your call but I'd like to know how you expect to perform in this state."

She looked up, not as high as his face but he felt her scrutiny somewhere around his breast bone, almost enough to rub the sting out with his palm. She was twisting him up somehow and he didn't like it. Some girls had a knack for it or maybe it was him. Honest? He had to stay away from girls of most kinds but especially this kind.

"Will you let me call a taxi?"

"What for?" *Why was he asking?* She was ready to get out of his way. He ought to be grateful but he kept thinking about her long, bare legs and wondering how her cropped hair would feel rubbing against his jaw. Or even better on his chest. Thick, brown, like a bear cub. *Was it soft, coarse, silky?*

"I have to get to the theater."

"When?"

"In an hour. The afternoon matinee."

He should have handed her the phone. He should have backed off. "Where is this theater?"

"Up the hill. The one that delivery van slid down yesterday."

He remembered. Cobbled street, forty-five degree angle, heavy load—bound to be trouble. No casualties, plenty of panic. "The police have closed it to traffic."

"I still have to get there." She slid her foot into the shoe again.

"I'll take you." *What? Am I crazy?*

The girl put the broken shoe on the other foot. "No traffic, remember?"

"Doesn't apply to my vehicle." He shrugged out of his high visibility jacket, ran his fingers through his hair.

"What's special about your car?"

"You'll see." Not exactly a ride a normal guy was proud to offer a girl.

Jakki hobbled after him, lop-sided in her fashionista outfit and top-notch field dressing. Mike growled out his destination and strode toward the Princes Street entrance to the site. At the gate, he caught sight of a roadster, but couldn't swear he recognized the driver. Jakki came up behind him. After a moment, he saw no sign she had seen the roadster.

"The ground's pretty bad here." With no warning, he picked her up and deposited her on the passenger seat of the construction site buggy.

"This is it?"

"If by 'it' you mean my vehicle, yes. Goes anywhere."

"Quaint."

No doors, but a hood over the cab, no windscreen. A stick shift with two forward gears and reverse. In no time, she learned the gears were forward slow and forward slower. One reverse at a crawl.

"Any problems?"

"Seat belt?"

"Dangling down there. Might have been torn off when I rolled it last week."

"Do you roll it often?"

She glanced above her to the solid roll bar, scratched and chipped, undented. Slender neck, delicate chin bone and skin as translucent as pearls.

"Only on weekends," he laughed. He jammed the gear shift forward and eased the buggy across the pavement, avoiding as many tourists as there were cracks in the street. "What kind of performance is this? What's the name of the play?"

"It's new. You won't have heard of it."

"Try me." That old shot of steel along his shoulders told him to back off. *Not worth it.* She tugged at her straight skirt, covering her knees and a pink mark just at the side that reminded him of a swirl of raspberry jam in ice cream. *Worth it.*

Damn. How many times did a guy get incinerated before he learned this code?

"What's your name?"

"Mike." For the third time, he said his name. The dark pink swirl peeked out at him as she turned, joined by a speck of blueberry on her thigh and a long, graceful sweep of chocolate that enticed his gaze to the hem of her tight skirt. He shifted gears, got his head out of that part of her anatomy quick before he drove the buggy into a gaggle of his fellow Americans. Tourists. What made them so crazy about these bloody whining pipes? Every summer. Like sheep, endless streams of wannabe Scots. "Where're you from?"

"I live in Musselburgh."

He nodded once, took the turn up the grade. That wasn't what he asked but he didn't want to hear her life story. He was only thinking about following swathes of chocolate. Hot chocolate. He banked the buggy wheels at the kerb in front of the sleaziest theater venue in that part of town. The marquee said it all. *Bondage.* Yeah. That's what it was all right. Dealing with girls with blueberry marks on their thighs. "Here ya go."

"Thanks."

"You going to be all right? Not dizzy?" Just let it go. She was already out of the buggy, wobbling a bit on her one stiletto and half a shoe. "Not performing in those, I hope."

"No." Her voice was not even a shadow.

"How long's the show?" *What? Why ask?*

"Ninety minutes."

The marquee gave the start time. Seven:ten. She'd be done by eight:forty. "Need a lift to Musselburgh?"

"I'll be okay. Thanks for offering."

"You know where I am."

"Yes." Girls like this stripped him bare and broke his back. He was done and she was a liar. There was no matinee. He'd had enough of girls like her in his life. There was something different about her. Something not quite right.

If not for the roadster slamming to a stop right next to his buggy….

No. He didn't want another man's discarded goods. He was done with junk yard sales.

two

Jimmy stood outside the Portacabin when Mike drove the buggy through the gate, bumping over the debris. The Scotsman shook his head but otherwise he had nothing to say.

Mike tossed his keys into the air and caught them behind his back, smug, satisfied with his decision to drive away from another disaster zone. After all, that was the reason he took this assignment—to get the hell as far away from girls who just didn't know when to quit. He was beaten down and battered but he wasn't out. Except for the peculiar craving for chocolate and raspberry swirl—hell, she did have nice legs.

What did he need with an actress or whatever she was, at his age, after what he'd been through with Margery? Enough grief to last another few years.

What he did want was a good night's sleep. Just one. That would be a good start. He slapped Jimmy on the back and slipped into the office.

Hell, what kind of guy shoves a wisp of a girl out of his car, shouting abuse for all the world to hear? What kind of girl goes around with a guy like that in the first place? He cleaned up all the bloody bandages and ointments, sat down at his desk to make a report. Damn. He hadn't thought about lawsuits but, yeah, she was the type to sue for damages to her stilettos. Mike worded his report with caution, putting his and his crew's action in the best possible light, made it clear she refused medical care.

Damn funny reaction to that young doctor. What got into her head about doctors, the hospital? She hid behind him. No other way to say it. He left that part out. She refused medical treatment. Concerned for her safety, he escorted her to her place of work. She was fine when he last saw her.

And I left her with the jerk who dumped her out of his car. He didn't write that. *Don't even want to think about it.* But there was no escape.

The crew were gone. Jimmy waited at the gate, the last to inspect the site for trespassers, indigents wanting a place to sleep or something to pawn.

"Time for a quick pint, Mike?"

"Not tonight."

"Hot date, eh?"

"You know me, Jimmy." Standing joke. Never a pint, quick or otherwise. Never a hot date. Jimmy went that way. Mike the other.

When he let himself into the flat, he dropped the keys on the table, already knowing he wasn't staying long. He drank a half pint of milk in one gulp from the bottle, showered and walked his bike out of the garage. He strapped the spare helmet on the pillion seat, shrugged and careened through the Fringe crowds back to Princes Street. Outside the make-do theater, he found a safe place to stow the bike and helmets, bought a ticket and sat at a table at the back.

He did not want to be doing this. He did not want to see this girl perform. He did not want anything to do with a production called *Bondage*. His gut was killing him. The cabaret atmosphere was a cheap trick. He bought a pint but let it go flat, warm. He'd never sleep after sitting in a wooden chair for ninety minutes. His leg was already cramping. The light went out. A few people used their mobile phones for a last bit of illumination before they were told to turn them off.

Nothing happened.

Chairs scraped. Someone coughed. Someone giggled. Still nothing. Mike groaned without making a sound. The blackout was solid. Before the audience had adjusted, a flick of a light let them see a girl where there hadn't been.

Not his girl. *His girl? Damn.* He was as good as chained, just a dumb junk yard dog. He crossed his arms, kept his balance, breathed through the pain, forgot about the show. When the lights came on again, he maneuvered his body to a standing position. Most of the audience ordered more drinks. Mike went to the stage and hooked his fingers at one of the actors.

"Jakki around?"

"Who wants to know?"

"Tell her Mike's here."

The actor disappeared. Mike worked to relax his lower back, subtle stretching that no one noticed. He was damned glad she wasn't in the show that night, wouldn't have known what to say if she asked him. All he'd done was keep from seizing up like an old man from the inactivity. He could have used another drink but he was driving back.

"Hi."

He lifted his eyes, staring at a green and orange striped knee. The other knee was pink and purple stripes. He raised his sites higher, the stripes came to the top of her knees, mid-thigh, above that, bare legs and a pair of black shorts. He just hoped he wasn't drooling. She wore gloves like the knee socks—thigh socks—no fingers in the gloves that reached above her elbows.

"Hi." His face was level with her ribcage. "I, uh, wanted to be sure you were okay."

"Thank you. I'm okay. Still a bit woozy."

"I didn't see you on stage."

"I wasn't allowed to perform."

"Probably for the best."

"Probably." But she didn't sound convinced. "Thank you for everything."

"Least I could do."

"Have you eaten yet?"

The thigh-high socks covered all the raspberry, blueberry and chocolate delights he spent the evening thinking about. Good thing. "There's a good place a few blocks over."

"Okay."

She made it sound like he'd asked her out. She was good, very good. The chain was getting tighter around his neck. Before long he'd be thinking about kissing her, wondering if she'd kiss him back.

"Can you walk in those shoes?"

She turned her foot this way and that, some sort of solid block of beige suede ankle boot with a wedge heel as high as his hand was broad. "Sure."

"Are you done here?"

She extended her hand for help down from the stage, leaned on his shoulder, wobbled a bit and smiled.

"The place isn't far but you might not want to walk."

"I can walk. And," she said, slipping her hand around his arm, "you'll be ready to catch me if I trip."

That was a clear prescription for the behavior she expected from him, so Mike took the hint. He'd be the guy who helped her walk in her crazy shoes.

She wore a fur waistcoat and a silk camisole. All bright, mismatched colors but all the craziness suited her.

"I want to have a look at your arm before we go anywhere." He peeled back the top of the glove. Something about doing that was like sliding a strap from her shoulder and he wondered how it felt to touch her without thinking about injuries and blood and field dressings. He held her arm gently, in the light from a wall lamp. People were finishing their drinks and gathering their coats. "Why weren't you allowed to perform?"

"With this big bandage on my arm?"

"You could have worn a long-sleeved blouse or these gloves."

"Out of character."

He hadn't seen any part of the play that couldn't have accommodated a long-sleeve or a glove. But, he hadn't

17

followed much of the story or made sense of the action. "You'll get another chance, won't you?"

"Not with this bandage."

He finished his examination and studied her face for a moment. "It's too soon to take this off, sorry. You'll pull the wound open."

"That's what I told Terry. He's not happy but I can't help that. He's never happy." Jakki shrugged her big bag onto her shoulder and clutched his arm. "Lead the way. I'm starving."

His first choice for dinner was packed with a line outside. "What do you want to do?"

"Isn't there a diner or café nearby? I told you I don't eat before a performance but I eat big time after."

"Another block okay for you?"

"As long as I can hang onto your arm, lead the way."

"Do you feel okay? Maybe we should take a cab or—."

"I can walk," Jakki said, "just not in these shoes."

"Why do you wear them?"

"I like them."

"It sure isn't for comfort." He opened the door of a Fifties-style diner, let her walk past him, watching how she teetered on the wedge heels, not awkward but with a sway that caught him off guard.

The waiter sent her in the direction of a booth and handed the menus to Mike. He wasn't surprised when the waiter's gaze followed her to the booth, but it wasn't because she looked good. When Mike passed him, the guy had a quizzical look on his face. *Tell me about it.* She turned heads all right. Weird clothes. Weird hair. Freaking high heels. She was tall enough barefoot to stand eye-to-eye with most any Scotsman he knew but in those things even he wasn't much taller.

Jakki ordered an American beer. He seconded the order.

"Just so you know, I don't pour my own drink."

Mike followed his short laugh with a twisted smirk and poured her beer. "Does that include wine or just the common stuff?"

"All drinks."

"Why's that?"

"Oh, just one of my quirks."

This girl had quirks all right. How many and how strange was anyone's guess. Mike contented himself with a long look but after a moment, she held out her hand, palm upwards. He laid the menu on her hand and dragged the other one toward him.

"Seems you'd better be happy with burgers. They don't do vegetarian."

"I eat meat," Jakki said, not looking up from her study. When the waiter came, she ordered a double cheese burger with fries and coleslaw. "I don't really like the way they serve coleslaw but I make do while I'm here. You know. Go native."

"Where're you from?" He didn't need to know. When she didn't answer right way, he let it slide again. She played with the cutlery and condiments, arranging and building haphazard and structured. "Another quirk?" he asked with a smile.

She lifted her head slowly and met his gaze. Tears threatened to spill out of her brown eyes but she checked them fast.

"You've had a rough day," he said, squeezing her fingers for a second. "Drink your beer, it's pretty good."

Jakki took a good gulp and slumped back. "You noticed."

"Hard to miss." He leaned forward, catching her gaze before she withdrew. "Who was that jerk?"

"Which one?"

She said it so seriously, he had to laugh. He sat back and admired her in a lot of funny ways. The whole look, the presence claimed consideration. Someone special. With quirks. "The one driving the roadster. The one who—."

"Don't remind me."

"That was a dangerous thing he did. Aren't you mad? Tell the police? Anything?"

She looked at him for several moments. He didn't flinch under her microscope nor did he break eye contact. Her eyes were focused on him as though she could read every thought in his head but even feeling that wasn't disconcerting enough to disconnect.

If she had taken a scalpel and slit him open from breastbone to belly, he did not want to evade her scrutiny. He never did, with any woman. Pointless effort, they always found what they were looking for, even if it wasn't there to begin with.

"You're a really nice guy, aren't you?"

He wasn't but that's what she wanted.

"I guess I didn't get the 'all men are jerks' memo." Just then he was thinking he wanted to kiss her. He already knew what and why. Soft with quirks. Tattooed? She was a likely candidate. He could live with that but he preferred the delights of raspberry swirls that every woman's body offered, no distractions.

"And," she said as if she could read his mind, "I always pay for my meal." In the next moment, she added, "Saves misunderstandings."

"No problem," he laughed, making room for the platter the waiter set in front of him. Jakki had already reached for mustard. Mike looked at her for a second. "You're not Scottish, are you?"

"No. Are you?"

"Pretty obvious I'm a Yank," he said with a grin. He waited for her to respond but she had tucked into the burger and made no sign she was about to reveal her nationality. With a shrug, he slapped the bottom of the ketchup bottle and salted the chips that passed for fries.

When she'd told him she ate "big time" after a performance, she hadn't exaggerated nor did she demure in actuality. She devoured every mouthful, morsel and crumb with pure pleasure in the taste of the food. Watching her eat was a pleasure. She made eating look like an exercise in bliss. If he got lucky that night, it wasn't because he'd paid for her meal. If he was *that* lucky, he'd be surprised.

Paying for her own meal was a statement, gave her complete freedom to enjoy, eat as much or as little as she wanted, of whatever she fancied. Another quirk. He got that message. Coming to terms with this girl's quirks was another unexpected pleasure. But something didn't gel with seeing her slammed on the pavement in front of him. Could be she didn't want anything to do with him. Could be he was hankering after something he wasn't going to get any closer to than he ever had before. Could be she was particular about some things and not others. Chances were he'd never know.

He drank his beer and watched her spoon Hot Fudge Sundae with extra caramel sauce into her mouth and savor the taste with her eyes closed, humming with each mouthful, driving him crazy thinking about kissing the tiny drop of caramel on her lip, licking it away and following that with tasty kisses wherever he could find blueberries and chocolate and her creamy skin. He was in deep trouble.

"Want some?"

"What?"

"Do you want some of my ice cream?"

"No, thanks." What was he thinking, turning down an offer of anything even remotely connected to what he wanted? "Doctor's orders." *Lame, Michael. Too lame for words. Quit while you've got some credibility.* "Ready to go?"

"Okay. I'm stuffed." She patted her tummy and giggled. When the waiter brought the check, she did a quick calculation and slid a twenty pound sterling bill across the table to him.

He laid another twenty on top and crawled out of the booth, wincing at the perpetual stab of pain he did his best to ignore.

"Are you okay?"

"Old war wound," he quipped, knowing she'd get it. Old guy, seizing up in his dotage. Barely in his thirties and he was past it. "Do you want a lift home or have you got that covered?"

"I'll take a lift if you're offering." She took his arm, leaning a bit into him.

He crooked his arm, clamped his elbow to his side as they came out onto the busy street. Fringe tourists and patrons

21

strolled up and down, across and through traffic as though there were no cars or buses. The natives hated every minute, took the money and played their bag pipes incessantly, that same droning, whining overcurrent every time a man came out of a door.

He'd taken time to shower and change but he still wore his scuffed construction boots—good substitute for motorcycle boots but no fashion statement. A sidelong glance assured him Jakki was enjoying the party. He was going to get her home and call it a night. Quits. It just didn't make sense to keep hanging around her like a junk yard dog.

"Sometimes, when I look over the edge and see all these people, I wonder what it's about. What I'm doing here."

Mike covered her hand and maneuvered her to the other side of his body, away from the kerb. Gradually, he wove through the throng toward the shop fronts so she wasn't bumped by drunken kilt-hangers and ignorant tourists.

He should have done better research when he took this assignment, turned it down on grounds of craziness, interference, undo stress. What had been a six-month tour had become more than a year. He was accustomed to the bagpipes, hardly heard them dawn to dusk but when they invaded the summer nights, they just added more irritant to his sleeplessness.

He was running out of painkillers and Dr. Kanipataraja was cutting his dosage, one refill of his prescription at a time.

"Why are we here?" The makeshift theater was deserted.

"I'm giving you a lift."

"Where's your buggy?"

He nodded in the direction of an alley and left her at the entrance. After he'd checked the bike over, he wheeled it back to the street and dropped the kickstand. When he saw her expression, he said, "It's safe and I don't take chances." Not so much a case of didn't as couldn't. "I've got all the gear you'll need." He popped the cargo lids, pulling out padded overalls and leather jacket. "Put these on. I don't want any more scrapes and scratches on you." He talked like a fourteen year old, saying stupid stuff and blushing. Blushing!

Jakki teetered under the weight of the leather gear. "I'll need some help with this, Mike." She held it out to him, along with what looked like a carpetbag.

He set the bag and jacket on the bike seat and beckoned her over to him. She took mincing steps on the cobbles. *Who in their right engineering mind left cobbles on a hill this steep?* Even worn flat, they were slick. He opened the zippers at the ankles and up the front, handed the garment back. She teetered from one foot to the other to get her balance right. She moved up close to him and turned her back, used him to lean on like a wall. A hard, solid wall. Crazy. *One of us is crazy and it ain't her.*

Once her feet were in the legs, she wriggled into the rest, slid the straps over her shoulders and turned for him to zip up the front.

He killed time to get his hands steady, worked the heavy-duty zipper up, tucking her clothes out of the way as he went. He crouched to zip the ankles, hoisting the pant legs up but they covered her shoes anyway. He lifted his head to look at her and there she was smiling at him, like she knew what she was doing to him.

Not going to happen, lady. He handed her the leather jacket, thrust the second helmet in her arms and got on, adjusting his jeans to accommodate his equipment. He couldn't think of any girl who had worked him like this one. *Maybe one.* But that was another story, all the wrong reasons. Over his shoulder he checked her progress with the helmet. "Get on."

She used his shoulder for a handhold, slid her left leg over the pillion and wriggled some more. Wriggled a lot.

He ignited the engine, made some adjustments, planted his boots on the cobbles.

"You'll have to stow that bag, balance is off."

Like she was made of nothing but supple ligaments, she drew her leg way back and stuffed the oversized bag in the cargo box and wriggled down until her legs were right up against his. He didn't have to tell her to hold on. Her arms were clenched around his chest so tight it wasn't only lust that made it hard for Mike to breathe.

Keeping his word about chances, he zig-zagged down the hill and slipped into traffic toward the castle. At the next light, she tapped his helmet.

"Have you been up there?"

He nodded. Requisite visitor site. His mother would never let him forget it if he hadn't sent her a souvenir.

"I'd like to see it. I've been here a month, just rehearsing and performing. Doesn't look like I'll see anything." She made herself more comfortable, moving her legs along his, pulling closer so he could feel her settling against his tailbone. Coccyx. He almost laughed.

At the next light, he turned left, then right onto the castle road.

"Thank you," she whispered against his neck.

Sucker. He backed the bike into a space and shut down the engine, wishing he could do the same. "Go ahead. I'll wait."

Jakki's head jerked up from the job of unzipping the jacket. "Okay."

If she had started to cry, her disappointment couldn't have been any more obvious.

"What?"

"Nothing. I won't be long."

"What's wrong?" Fool for asking. He unbuckled the strap and yanked off his helmet, set it on the horn of the seat for concealment. "Do you want me to walk up there with you?" Double fool for handing her the stick.

"Would you?"

Resigned to his fate.

three

The optimum word was 'used.' They went through the same routine of using him for balance to get her out of the overalls and using him to walk up the grade to the entrance and using him to climb the stairs, any stairs; using him to keep warm on the wall so she could watch all the lights in the city twinkle. But there was no way in a frosty Edinburgh summer night he was going to have a chance at using her except to get more worked up.

She compelled him to wrap his arms around her at the highest viewing spot, wriggled into his jacket while he was still wearing it, wrapping it around her as if she owned it and resting the back of her head on his collarbone. Proprietary.

He stuffed his hands in his pockets. At least he was a volunteer in his own downfall. He may have been a silent, passive witness but he wasn't falling. No surrender. He wasn't going to make the mistake of assumption. This girl had too many unknown blind corners and there was no way he was getting himself trapped in any of them. No panting at her heels. No begging for scraps. Not this time. Never again.

Whatever her game, he had to admit he hadn't felt this good in a long time. Whatever else was going on, he hadn't felt anything near as good with a woman, in a woman's company, for years. Maybe she was playing him. Maybe she was marking him out for something but he liked this presumption of right she assumed. He didn't mind being used. It wasn't as if she could hurt him. Not as if he hadn't been used up and spit out often enough.

"Are you going to tell me where you're from?"

"Will it make any difference?"

"Any difference to what?"

"To whether you like me?" She turned her head and tilted back to look up at him, just enough so her lips were a fraction below his jaw.

"No," he said, barely moving his mouth so he wouldn't accidently feel her lips on his chin. He tilted his head back to look at the sky just in case. "It's not as if this is going to last."

"No?" She unwrapped herself from his jacket and leaned instead on the balustrade.

The north wind blew hard against his chest without her warmth and whipped her fur waistcoat like nothing more substantial than tissue paper. He wanted her back but there was no chance he was going after her.

"Hey, do you want to go dancing? I know a great place."

"I was giving you a lift home."

"Okay. If that's what you want. This is a hoot. Like nothing else. Just for the Fringe."

"What sort of dancing?" That blasted chain just got tighter. As soon as this girl showed any level of enthusiasm, he wanted it. He wanted to soak in the animation, the pure joy she exuded.

"You'll see!" She took his arm and wriggled in front of him, encouraging him to follow, to join her, to play.

He caved. He took one step and she laughed, so full of life he had to clamp himself down to keep from throwing his arms around her and kissing her like he'd never kissed anyone ever before in his life. He wanted whatever she was dishing out.

She tugged him all the way back to his bike, made him stand still, keep his hands to himself, slid behind him and sank into his body like a down comforter.

They rode north. She tapped his helmet when she wanted him to turn, moving her hand in slow motion in his peripheral vision. He pulled up outside a Presbyterian church and she was off the bike and stripping out of the leathers faster than a firecracker.

"You'll love this. Come on!" She was on his arm again, propelling him up the stairs, around the back, through a narrow door and into a hall filled with people of all ages, dressed in whatever, dancing like maniacs to music he hadn't heard since he left home.

"Swing? You like big band swing?"

"Sure! This is the greatest. You can't help but dance." She pulled his jacket off his shoulders and swayed in time to the music.

Mike tossed his jacket toward a chair along the wall and put his arm out. Jakki wriggled into it and dropped her arms over his shoulders, her hands dangling behind his neck. Mike set his hands on her waist and, in spite of his reservations, all the years of watching his parents swing to Goodman and Dorsey and picking up great moves from his dad came back, slamming into him like the Chattanooga Choo-Choo on Track Twenty-nine. He hadn't had more than twelve ounces of beer but he felt no pain. He hadn't had this much fun since before the night he was dragged across half a football field of highway.

He didn't know the time or much care. He wasn't going to sleep even when he did get back to the flat so he couldn't much complain if she kept him out all night.

"Hey, you can dance," she said. "I mean really dance."

"Inbred." He put his arm around her and took her hand, leading the way to the middle of the dance floor to the mellow sounds of Glenn Miller and danced with her until the end of the last recording and the dancers were gathering up their coats. Still reluctant to let her go, he dropped his arms as the lights overhead came on.

"Time to go."

He nodded, not surprised that she sounded as enthusiastic about ending as she was about starting.

Mike scooped up his jacket, felt the familiar twinge in his back but shrugged it off, offering Jakki his arm as they filtered out of the church hall. "How did you find out about this place?"

"It's in the Fringe event guide. I made a list of everything I wanted to do. Just in case I was free."

"Where to now?" Chances were fair she'd have something else on her list.

"As much as I'd like to go on, you have to get to work in the morning and I need to rehearse. We both have jobs to do."

Gutted. Sucker punch. Walked right smack into that one. On went the leathers and the helmet, up went the overall zipper. Tap on his helmet, slow motion signals and they arrived at a row-house, stone-built, two-storey, two-up, two-down house, front garden could have done with a car on blocks for some style. All the lights were on, music and laughter from the open windows. She handed him the leathers, having no trouble keeping her balance while her fellow actors were watching.

"Thank you, Mike."

"Sure. Anytime." He was back on the bike, keeping his eyes off the front door, keeping his eyes on her, committing her to memory from the bear cub fur on her head to her mismatched striped stockings, crazy shoes, long legs. He stowed the leathers and spare helmet, stretched his back and lifted his helmet. "Keep your arm covered."

"I will."

Her friends called her in and she walked up the footpath without any help, no looking back and, by the time she was at the door, the construction site foreman who'd fallen in love with her had roared out of the street.

four

Another night of the television keeping him company while he waited for the painkillers to take the edge off. No big deal. Standing in the shower with his hands throttling the shower head while the hot water shot over his chest to ease *that* ache was new.

At least he hadn't made a complete jackass of himself. He hadn't asked to see her again, hadn't begged for her number, hadn't hinted he wanted an invitation to her room, no groping, no failed attempts to kiss her. Perfect gentleman. *Cool. Real cool.*

So why did he feel so lousy? He hadn't turned into the bozo she expected, didn't give her the satisfaction of bringing him to his knees. Hadn't committed any sin or compromised his sense of honor. So why was he kicking himself?

He lay down in the middle of the bed so he kidded himself. Less obvious he was sleeping alone, dragged the duvet over his legs, tossed it off when even that weight cramped his muscles. No opportunity to dream about long-legged girls in long gloves—he didn't sleep. He didn't have to dream, he couldn't get her out of his head.

Painkillers didn't work to take *that* edge off. He was hard and she was probably soft for one of those guys waiting for her at the door. All good looking, younger than him. Maybe one of them drove a roadster. Did she go back to the jerk after taking *him* for a ride? Was she telling that jerk about the junk yard dog, panting at her heels, begging for scraps?

So what? It wasn't as if he'd never been laughed at before. Take it for what it was. Like he said, it wasn't as if it was ever going to last. *She's never going to know you fell for her.* Not for sure. He'd played his part cool and close. She had no sure thing evidence he was smitten. He wished the hell he wasn't.

Then came the devil. Hope. Imagining how he'd turn his head and see her next to him, seeing all the raspberry, blueberry and chocolate in obscure places that no one else noticed, following their clues wherever they led him. Her bare, creamy legs were his guide to what the rest of her might be like once he—if only.

At 6AM, he took another shower, put on his work clothes and walked to the diner on Dougall to have breakfast. The waitress gave him a smile. He managed to give one back, read the local rag and walked the rest of the way to the construction site.

His crew hadn't arrived. He stomped dust off his boots and unlocked the office, tossed his jacket—he'd have to have it cleaned to get rid of that female scent. Couldn't have Jimmy finding any evidence to fuel his ridicule. He exchanged the jacket for his high visibility vest, walked onto the site and made plans for the work that day.

"Good night?" Jimmy bounced into his field of vision at six:forty-five. The rest of his crew were walking through the gates with a few stragglers coming up the street from the bus stations.

"Usual." Mike tilted his hard hat back from his forehead. "We're clear to start work on the pour. No rain predicted."

"Right, Mickey." Jimmy made no move to set his men to work. "Did you no' see that lass—. I mean t'say, I wonder how the lass is doing after that fall."

Jimmy knew him pretty well, knew he would check up on her, just to be sure she was all right. "She was fine when I dropped her off at her boyfriend's place." That would settle it. No opening for jokes or speculation.

"And when would that ha' been, Mickey?"

Mike flared, stopped himself from the defense, took the offense. "After dinner and a dance or two."

Jimmy slapped him on the back, whistled and walked away. Done deal. He didn't hear any more about the lass, from Jimmy or any of the crew. He got on with his job.

By noon, he hadn't given any thought to the lass any more than twenty times. An improvement on the twenty times an hour it had been since he last saw her. The affect was wearing off; he hadn't lost his ability to compartmentalize, concentrate on his job. The men brought out their lunch boxes.

Jimmy took a walk to get some "Air that's no' filled with dirt." Mike used the Portaloo and washed his hands in the spigot, cursing when soapy water splashed his boots.

"Hey."

He straightened his back, slow and easy, stared through the chainlink fence. Big sunglasses. Big green ribbon tied around her head with a big bow. He couldn't help smiling. She was all about statement.

"They won't let me in."

"This is a construction zone. Hard hat area."

Purple sundress to her knees. And greenish shoes more like stilts. "I brought your lunch." The bow and the stilettos didn't match. Both really ugly greens. The bow like pea soup. The stilts like day-glow tennis balls. He was happy to see her.

"Wait there." He walked around the pilings, enduring the crew's stares and grins.

"Jimmy's going to kick himself for missing this."

Mike pushed back his hard hat, took it off as he left the site, rubbed the band marks out of his hair, could feel the grit on his forehead and nose.

"I figured I owed you a real thank you for fixing my arm."

"How does it feel today?"

"Bit sore. Scratchy."

"Means it's healing."

She held out a lunch box, brand new, fashion statement style, bit girlie for a construction worker. He smiled and offered his arm. She clasped it, stroked his forearm with fingers half-covered with yellow, fingerless hand-warmers. Her bandaged arm was covered by a scarf.

"I think you should look at it."

"I think you should have it checked by a doctor."

"You'll do fine." She gave his arm a quick hug and took off in the direction of the site gate.

Before any of the crew saw him he returned the lunch box. She swung it at the end of her arm like a school bell, swaying on her beacon stilts and flashing big smiles at the six men gaping at her and their site manager.

"Guess Jimmy's no' going to miss a thing."

Jakki climbed the cabin steps ahead of Mike, skirt swinging, glimpses of swirls and swoops leading in directions he ached to visit. Inside, she set the lunchbox on his desk, openly examining his papers and files, desk calendar. Nothing incriminating to catch her attention. She unknotted the silk scarf and peeled it off one wind at a time, keeping her eyes on her victim.

The oddity of the striptease wasn't lost on Mike. He watched. She let the orange silk slide from her fingers onto his files. When she offered her arm to him, he stepped forward.

Two could play. His was not going to be the only unrequited ache in the room. He sat on the edge of the desk and eased her between his knees holding her arm steady, with her wrist trapped against his ribs. With one hand cupped around her elbow, he worked the adhesive loose at the top of the gauze and leaned enough to put her off balance as he tossed the sticky bandage toward the rubbish bin, keeping her upright with his thighs.

She was killing him with submission. She smelled like honey. And lemons. Warm and clean. He was killing himself with speculation. He guessed she wore Brazilian panties, maybe French. Not a thong. She'd go for subtle, with lace. She wore a bra, doubted it matched her panties but she might surprise him.

Yeah, as if he was going to have the privilege of finding out. Could happen, if he played well. He unwound the gauze once, gathered the fabric, caressing her skin with his fingers, unwound more, caressed the smooth, peach-white naked flesh, felt her flinch. Good sign. Another lean. Another caress. Skin, sun-warmed, soft as a baby. His eyes were locked on his job but his peripheral vision caught the fingers of her free hand wavering between staying at her side and reaching for support. She was warm. He was combusting.

Half-rising, he found the bandage scissors. When he sat down, he moved enough so she straddled his thigh. She caught her breath. Her fingers played at the front of her dress. He flexed the muscles of his thigh. She wriggled. He eased the scissors, cold stainless, up her arm. A snip. Ease. Another snip. Easy. Easy. Slice and she was exposed. He inhaled, pulled her injured arm closer, clamping her bare leg between his knees, unbalancing her just a bit so she grazed his upper thigh and put herself right. Fast.

Almost there. He leaned back to grab the first aid kit and she toppled off the stilts, all that softness in touch with unyielding muscle and denim. Her breath came shallow and fast. He eased her upright, focused on her arm, at the same time clenching his thigh, her heat rising like the morning sun.

"Are you done?"

"Almost," he answered, sliding his leg forward so she had no choice but to ride him. All the time, he focused on the treatment. Her arm mostly. Her free hand braced on his shoulder, fingers stretching. "There. All done." He put his tools away, relaxed all his muscles. "Feel any better?"

"A little."

"Hungry?"

"Are you?"

"Starving," he admitted, taking the lunchbox to the office sofa. "You'll still feel a little sore. Scratchy. But that will go away in a few days. It's a clean wound. No infection."

"So no reason to see a doctor." She hadn't turned from the desk.

"None I can see."

She studied her arm. "Will it leave a scar?"

"A small one. But that will fade over time."
"No lasting damage."
"None."

five

Feeling lousy was a perpetual aftermath of Mike's encounters with this girl. Sure, he'd had his brief victory, succeeded in leaving her with a sense of the frustration he felt but he didn't feel good about it. He escorted her off the site with a lighter dressing and a sincere thank you for providing him with a gourmet lunch but, whatever satisfaction he had, evaporated when she hailed a cab, was driven off to her performance and he realized she was going to climb that cobbled hill in those yellowy green stilts.

He tried the 'Not my problem' get-out clause all afternoon but it didn't wash the bad feeling out. He pulled at the collar of his chambray shirt as if he could loosen the choke chain but that didn't help. He sat on his bike outside the *Bondage* venue with his helmet on his lap until the last of the audience was gone and the lights went out above the entrance.

The actors came out from the alley in groups of twos and threes, passing him with a glance, tripping, stumbling and laughing as they went. He recognized most of them, not from the performance but from the flat the night before.

"Hey."

He turned his head.

"I didn't expect to see you." She hung onto some kid's arm. Didn't think twice about kicking a junk yard dog in the belly. She let the kid go.

"You coming, Jakki?" the kid asked.

"You go ahead."

The kid gave Mike a narrowed-eyed stare. A sharp 'Boo' crossed Mike's mind but he held back. She wobbled one step toward him. That didn't mean she'd picked him over the kid.

"We'll wait for you at the club."

She nodded.

"Don't bother," Mike said, handing over the leathers, holding her around the waist while she struggled into the legs, catching the heels of her ugly yellowy green shoes, stepping on the bottoms when she pulled them up, hitching the skirt of her dress in the back, trapping the front in the zip. Mike took pity on her and finished the job, keeping his hands from straying. Not easy. "Did you perform tonight?"

"Yes."

"Good show?"

"The audience was happy."

"Were you?"

"Out of sorts."

"You've had a rough time. Don't be too hard on yourself."

"Tell that to the director." She slid her arms into the jacket.

When she faced him, he caught the bottom and closed the zipper. "It's cold where we're going."

She didn't ask or protest. Acquiescent in a way that was diametrically opposed to her behavior the night before. Winding him up and around a finger she didn't even have to twist to catch his attention. He was riveted solid, like a cross beam to an eye beam. Anytime soon he'd trip up, fall flat on his face.

"Did you want to join your friends? I can drop you off if you'd rather." Best he could do to fake disinterest.

"Where are you going?"

"I'm open but since you told me you didn't have time to see much, I thought you'd like a tour. I know it's dark but there are some great streets among these hills. Historic. Sentimental. Picturesque." He reached inside his jacket, about to blow his cover. "I bought these postcards so you could see what these places look like in daylight."

"That's—. Thank you." She held the postcards against her heart for a moment.

"Hop on. I'm no tourist guide but I've discovered a few places, off the usual trail."

Jakki settled behind him, wrapped her arms around his chest and planted her chin on his shoulder. He tapped her helmet, slalomed down the hill and took a left. She nestled up against him, felt so good he was content to ride through the crowded streets, savoring she chose to be with him, before he offered anything.

Maybe she was beautiful in ways he hadn't discovered. Maybe she was smarter than she looked. For certain, he was hooked whatever way it went.

At Haymarket, he stopped at the kerb, under a lamp post and riffled through the cards she had slipped into his breast pocket. He handed her one.

"This is the largest auction house in the world. Forget Sotheby's and Christie's. More works of art, antiques and jewels change hands at the Haymarket than all those places combined. One of the most noteworthy buyers was William Randolph Hearst. Some of the treasures at his San Simeon castle were bought here." The bike engine hummed.

She took off her helmet to study the photo card. Mike caught the green bow before it fell to the muddy street, slipped it into his pocket for safe keeping. She turned the card over to read and glanced up at him.

"The card didn't give much away," he said, revving the engine. As if she didn't already know he was on the hook and all she had to do was crank him in.

Jakki put the card back with its companions and slapped her helmet in place. When she adjusted her position, she laid her head on his shoulder and held him low around his hips. *Maybe.* Maybe he wasn't the only one getting reeled in. He adjusted his position, avoiding the contact, avoiding the discomfort of possibilities. *This can't go anywhere, bozo.*

Up Leith Walk, passing Picardy Place, he took the hill, careful on the damp surface, and stopped at the roundabout. Easing forward as the traffic swished past to his right, from nowhere, a car cut across from the left lane and shot into the circle. Mike swerved, lost it and ran up onto the pavement, finally stopping perpendicular to the door of a café.

"Bastard. Are you okay?"

She didn't answer, but hung onto him, quiet and trembling.

"I forgot. You're probably hungry, right?"

"Yes."

He helped her off and pushed the bike onto the road. "There's no way he didn't see——." He caught her hands and put his arm around her shoulders. "Leave the gear on. Let's get inside." Her face was ashen in the florescent light. Mike helped her out of the jacket and dropped his over the back of his chair. "I know," he said with a grin, "I'll pour your drink and pay for my own meal."

Her gaze dropped to stare at the table. She didn't play with the cutlery or the condiments.

"I'm from San Francisco."

He relaxed back in his chair, staring at the top of her head. As they said in this neck of the woods, *'Result.'* Not ground breaking. Not earth moving, but a nudge in the direction of *'Getting to know you, getting to know all about you'* from his mother's favorite movie. Any moment, he'd start singing, Marni Nixon's voice-overs rattled around in his head with Deborah Kerr's face attached. Mike dropped his gaze, fumbled for one of the menus, when Yul Brynner opened his mouth. *'A Puzzlement'* wasn't even the half of what Mike thought at the moment.

"Great place," he replied, once he'd cleared his five-year-old sick-at-home with his movie-mad mom experience out of his skull.

The girl across the table nodded and reached for another menu.

Six

Forty-five minutes later, he held her hand as they walked out of the café. She paid for her late night breakfast, he paid for his cheeseburger and poured her coffee. What could he expect for a first date? The night before didn't count. They were in new territory.

"Is that church holding a dance tonight?"

"No. It's only one night a week."

Mike made a note of which night and pushed his helmet down. She climbed behind him, settled in the way he liked, held tight, tighter. Head down. Maybe she was watching the sights to the side or wasn't all that interested.

For what it was worth to him, Mike was content either way but he wanted her to enjoy the few hours he could spend with her, whatever it meant. If he—*scratch that. When* he was honest, and he often was, just being around this crazy lass gave him something to hanker for. He hadn't paid much attention to the Fringe, except as a gross annoyance, but he'd done his research and knew he had less than seven days to make any progress.

Whoever the roadster jerk was, he'd done Mike a favor, and a massive disservice. At the roundabout below John Lewis, he planted his boots on the road, searched in all directions before he throttled forward and halted again as a bus came up the hill. Behind the bus, a car tailgated, revving its engine, shot past into the circle and cut the bus off. Outraged, the bus driver shook his fist and shouted, "Indicators!" as only a Scotsman can.

Jakki flipped like a switchblade. Mike glared after the roadster, got the number on the license plate and rolled through the intersection, giving the bus driver a compassionate thumbs up. He'd lived in the area long enough to be familiar with the one-way system and tailed the roadster from a distance. He kept back until the roadster took a turn through an upmarket residential area. He dropped further back but it wasn't enough.

"What are you doing?"

He didn't want to lie. He didn't want to tell her the truth either. After another few blocks, she tapped his helmet.

"Where are we going?"

"There's a site over here."

"I don't want to go."

"I'll just—."

"Stop. Stop now." She wasn't screaming at him but when he didn't stop, she slapped his helmet, hard. "Stop. Stop. Stop," hitting his helmet and getting louder with each word. "Please stop. Please stop."

When she yanked on his shoulders, Mike eased up on the throttle, slammed his boots on the asphalt and ripped his helmet off. "What's wrong with you?"

Her expression told him everything. Everything was wrong with her. All her quirks and crazy clothes and dangerous footwear said everything.

"I wanted you to stop."

"You could have—. I could have lost control. We could be dead."

"Why did you do that?"

"What? Do what?"

"Follow him. Why did you follow him?"

"That's the jerk who—."

"It wasn't his fault." Jakki slid off the pillion and stood facing the street, arms folded around her chest. She wobbled but not because of her crazy shoes. "It's me. It's my fault. Always."

"How? How can something like what he did be your fault?"

"It is. It's just the way I am."

"That's crazy. I saw what happened. You didn't jump from that car."

"I'm to blame. I'm always to blame."

This was a new one on him. If anyone was at fault, he had always been assured it was the man's fault. More precisely *his* fault. He smoothed his hands over his thighs, resting them above his knees. "So this guy gets away with causing serious bodily harm because you made him mad."

"He wasn't mad."

"What's his excuse? Provocation?" Margery's favorite excuse for slamming him, throwing him out, taking a swing at his head with whatever she was holding. The steam iron hurt the worst. His jaw clenched. His eyes rolled and slammed shut. *Man.*

"I'd like to go."

"Hop on." He slid the helmet over his head, fastened the strap. She slid behind him but held away, placed her hands on his waist. He rolled away from the kerb and returned to the main street. He wasn't finished with Roadster Jerk but he had finished with asking Jakki questions about him or anything about her relationship with him.

At the main street through the west end of the city he resumed the ride to his intended destination. After a few silent stops at lights and past well-known landmarks, she relaxed enough to lean against him but he had lost precious ground with his venture to be a hero.

At the next light, he turned left and, at the narrow entrance, he turned right, cutting the engine and coasting to the end of an alley. He held her steady as she dismounted at the gate to a walled garden. Holding her hand on his forearm for a moment, he bent his head to look into her face. Though there was only a dim light over the gate, her face shone clearly as she met his gaze.

"I apologize. I had no right to make assumptions about what you wanted. And I do not need to know anything about him or what happened."

"I've been a celebrity since I was fourteen."

Okay. Maybe she was crazier than he thought. Maybe the Roadster Jerk had a point. Mike kept his gaze focused on her face, her whole face, not her eyes though they were filling with tears, waiting for an explanation, not expecting any clarification of her claim. He'd done it, worse than he wanted to admit. If she swung at his head, he figured he deserved it this time.

"I was already a curiosity. Everyone knew me. I wanted to be sure they knew me the way I decided, not because of what they imagined."

"So that explains what, darlin'?" Maybe he wasn't a dead man, maybe he wasn't out for the count.

"I decided, if I was going to be famous, I had to look the part. I had to be a celebrity on my terms, not theirs."

"You've done that for sure," Mike laughed, hugging her close. She melted into him for a moment and he choked on the chain, hanging on until she looked around the garden and smiled.

"How did you know I'd want to be here?"

"I guessed," he said, leading her through the entrance into Greyfriars Cemetery. The monument to the steadfast canine stood out among the stones and railings.

Jakki glanced at the statue once and went in another direction. Mike followed. The little he knew about this dame supported notoriety, possibly fame but there was nothing of the ordinary starlet about her.

When they reached the grave of the object of the little dog's loyalty, Jakki stood gazing at the tombstone in the dark. "What inspires that kind of love?"

"I'm a cynic, not the best person to answer that."

"What do you think?"

"The dog didn't know what else to do."

"So why are we here?"

"You're not a cynic."

"I'd be better off if I was," she said, bending to pluck a candy wrapper from the foliage around the grave. "Loads of other people are. Loads of people have done their best to encourage me to develop a cynicism skill."

"Like who?"

"You don't need to know." She tossed the wrapper in a trash bin, pulling a random postcard from his pocket. "Do we have time to go here?"

Mike peered at the photo of the public park near Princes Street. "We can do that tomorrow."

She didn't protest when he led the way to his bike and began the journey to Musselburgh. Her fellow actors were still in the city. Mike waited but she made no offers. "Good night," she said and walked toward the door. "Any requests for lunch?"

"Your choice." He rode out of the street. *Lunch. Tomorrow.* All good. He took the main road for a mile or so, then veered off to ride along the riverfront. Every inch was littered with tourists, lounging, drinking, laughing. Here he was. An itinerant worker from a small Pennsylvania town, meeting an American girl in a city overrun by American visitors, not one of them with any sense of how much their presence was resented and, at the same time, a necessary financial evil for the residents.

In a few days' time, most would be gone. The city would breathe a collective sigh and count the change, calculate the cost, start planning the same for two, three years ahead. Next year's Fringe already planned and advancing.

By then, he'd be gone. No idea yet where they'd choose to send him or where he'd elect to go—anywhere but Stateside, nowhere remotely like home. Maybe he'd book his parents a trip if he went someplace they'd want to visit.

He stopped by the river, watched it flow out to the North Sea, churning. Yearning, wanting, needing someone to love again. Churning him up inside. All that ache and glory and pain again. For what? He was good. Job. Place to live. Company when he wanted. What was he thinking? Not straight. That's for damn sure. Crooked as ever, all over again. The bike hummed all the way. Mike hummed along, pulled up and stared ahead. He didn't need his gut to tell him what to do. She didn't have to crank.

Fluffy, Pepto-Bismol pink socks. Bare legs. Purple dress. His leather jacket. Good thing his head was down or she'd see him grin. She stepped back into the narrow hallway. He stepped in.

"I'm not done." He wrapped her up in his arms and kissed her, still a silly grin on his face. She wasn't cold. Not resistant. Not wildly responsive but he didn't expect that. Not from her. Not yet. He could get her, bring her around to his level. He knew that. Good enough. She let him kiss her and keep on kissing her until he didn't need to kiss her like that anymore, until he could bring it down a notch, rev it down, stop churning, another notch, two, three down, until he was breathing.

"Good luck, mate. She'll suck you dry and leave you hanging."

The guy shoved past, knocking Mike's shoulder into the wall, tottering both of them off balance. She was on her toes. He staggered to keep on his feet. No time to react, to get the guy, make him explain, apologize. No time to see the guy's face.

She had the damnedest, staring, prettiest eyes, trained right on his face. He didn't need to know anything, looking into those eyes. He kissed her again, this time gentle, tentative, searching, gentle again.

She caught her breath when he pulled away.

"Guh nigh', lass," he said in his best Scots. He wasn't dry and he was by no means hanging. The nag in his back hit as soon as he sat on the bike saddle. He didn't look back to see if she was at the door, knew she wasn't.

seven

He grabbed the handrail in his building to get up the stairs, stood breathing heavy through the pain. When he could walk without feeling sick, he downed two tablets and a few pints of water. He braced his hands on the window frame as the city wound down.

Knowing by now he'd never get to sleep, he turned on the television, found a channel than didn't wind him up and strapped the back brace around his waist, took the green bow from his pocket and put it on the arm of the sofa. By the time the streets were empty of Fringe visitors, they were waking up to the milk floats, buses and baristas.

The shower spray hit him square in the face, ran down his chest, still hot over his groin. He hadn't let thoughts about the other guy anywhere near him all night but looking down at his equipment he recalled the prediction. Hanging, anyway. Thinking about her changed that but wondering about the prophecy won his attention while he ate his breakfast.

Dressed and ready to get to work, he stood where he could see the sun rising, wondering why he wasn't jealous. The guy knew something about Jakki, but he couldn't quite get a handle on it. He'd sensed it from the beginning, something about her that he was okay about. He wasn't done. He didn't feel lousy. He felt okay. He was handling all the surprises pretty well. He even liked it. He felt good about whatever the day might bring. He could handle it.

The phone rang before Mike had his key in the lock. Not good. The only callers were Head Office. Head Office only called when there was a problem. His crew hadn't missed a target date in the year he had been site manager.

"Where's the police report case number, Argent?"

Mike contained the long sigh that threatened to undermine his reputation.

"Give it to me and we'll do the follow up."

"I'll have to call you back."

"Listen, Argent. We don't have that kind of time. If the driver is a tourist at the bloody Fringe, we'll lose him. No chance to recover damages. You get it?"

"I get it, Ferguson."

"What's the update on the victim?"

"No serious injuries."

"We'll need a medical report on that."

"You won't get one."

"What?"

"The victim refused medical treatment."

"You're kidding me, right?"

When Mike remained silent, Ferguson banged the receiver on his desk. *Type A*. Mike relaxed back in his desk chair. "My report is good, I treated her—."

"Her? What the hell? That wasn't in your report, Mike. What are you playing at?"

"There's nothing on the form about that, Ferguson."

"Have you any idea how serious this is? You should have told me."

"I'm a trained medic. I treated the injury. Miss Hunter refused medical treatment. That's all in my report." Refused with a vengeance.

"Nothing about the victim being a woman."

"Look, Ferguson, I'll get you the police case number. Do what you want but Miss Hunter won't be suing Gregory and Bassett."

"And just how can you guarantee that?"

He couldn't and whatever he said was a guarantee of more hassle from Ferguson. "I can. I've got work to do. Jimmy will give you the case number when he gets in." He dropped the receiver on the cradle and greeted his subordinate with a roll of his eyes. "Get on it, will you, Jimmy?"

"Aye, that I will, Mike, but it will no' be popular with your lass, y'know."

"She doesn't have to know." *Your lass.* He liked the sound of that.

"She will. Y'can count on it."

"I should have made the report right then. Distracted."

"Canna' say I blame yuh. From what I've been hearing, you're doing all right."

"Here's the report. See to the police, please. When you have a number, let Ferguson know."

"He'll find out yuh didna' report it 'til today, y'know."

"Can't help that, Jimmy."

"Sure as hell the lass must be worth it, Mickey. But you're gonna need a good solicitah on your side."

Mike shrugged into his high visibility vest and hooked the hard hat with a finger as he walked onto the site.

"An' I got the best there is for yuh. She'll do right by yuh for sure." Jimmy followed him to the deck, shaking his head. "Mary McEwan, Mickey. Remember the name."

Mike waved without looking back, in no mood to discuss the night before or anything Ferguson was riled about. There was everything and nothing to play for—a good chance he'd blown it all with that wild move. Off the game plan and out of character, real fifteen year old kid's move. The one good thing was he'd gotten a kiss, reciprocated to an acceptable degree, something to build on.

The morning went. Lunchtime came and went. He bought a burger and coffee, not thinking about what he'd expected, hoped. Told himself he needed his head examined. Ferguson showed his face in the afternoon, a few minutes short of quitting time. The two bulky men squared off in the office. Ferguson demanded an explanation.

"You've screwed up big time, Argent. This is going against you."

"I made a thorough report. Miss Hunter made it clear she wasn't pressing charges against the driver."

"Not good enough. At least Jimmy had the sense to get the report in within a couple days or we'd be screwed. Were you thinking with anything above your tool belt?"

"Just because there's a woman involved—."

"Don't give me any lame defense. Jimmy told me this Hunter woman's an actress." Ferguson leaned forward. "You don't know anything about these Fringe types. Obviously got her hooks in you already."

"She's not like that."

"Know her pretty well, do you?"

Mike shook his head a moment. "What of it? She's an okay kid."

Ferguson swore under his breath. "I thought you were smarter. After that hit and run and your wife running out on you—."

Not even close to the way it really went down. No one knew that story. His own personal hell bent for leather tale he'd never tell. "Nothing to do with it, Ferguson."

"Like hell." Ferguson slapped his palm on his forehead. "Look, every man has a right to a good time if he can get it but these Fringe people aren't anything like us. Watch yourself, Mike."

"I've been around awhile, Pete. I know a bad show when I see one." First name basis. That hadn't happened before. *What does he know?* Not hard to guess from the pissed-off look in Pete Ferguson's eyes. *Been there.* "I know you're hacked off because of this police report. I'll set the record straight the next time I see Miss Hunter. Make it clear what has to happen."

"Anytime soon, Argent, is already late."

"I get it."

Before Mike left the site, Jimmy slapped a business card against his belly.

When Mike parked his bike and walked up the hill to the theater, he had an excuse for putting himself in a bad place. That didn't change how lousy he was feeling. Just one show. A short discussion. Job done.

He paid the admission, found a table far enough away from the stage to go unnoticed, ordered a drink from a smiling waitress and convinced his back it could relax. His back didn't agree and he sat upright, stretching his muscles whenever they screamed at him. No change.

He was driving, no painkillers, no knock-out drinking. He was set for a bad time on all levels, couldn't even depend on the performance to divert his attention. He flipped the business card back and forth. *Mary McEwan, Attorney at Law.* Mike shrugged, returning the card to his breast pocket.

A few more people in the audience than his first time but not enough for the backers to break even. Tax write-off for them.

Audience coughing. Laughing. Scraping their chairs. Clinking jewelry. Phones vibrating. *Why do they come?* Cheap booze. Provocative title. Not sleazy enough to get crowds. Some switched their phones off. Some only put them on silent. Not important enough to warrant full attention. Crackling chips bags. The same kind of people who left candy wrappers on graves. The same kind of people who trash the streets, expecting the Scots to clean up after them.

No respect for the actors. Something to do while they were in town. Mike dug in his pocket and turned off his phone, smirking at the dark screen. Empty gesture. No one ever phoned him.

He hadn't seen the play since the night Jakki wasn't allowed to perform, wasn't prepared when she danced on stage and took the downstage right position. Never still for a moment. He couldn't take his eyes off her. He heard voices, sound effects, screams, laughter but, at the end of the performance, he had no clue what the production was about.

She moved as though she had no solid bone in her body. Fluid. Subtle. Every fragment a part of the integrity of the whole. He doubted there was even one man in the audience who hadn't been watching and thinking exactly what he was thinking. Not thinking. Right in it. Living it. Wanting it.

The applause was warm, generous, tapering off to polite and dropping sharp when the dancer didn't show to take her bow.

He gave thanks in silence he didn't have to endure the gawking, fawning and panting of the other junk yard dogs in that dingy room. He didn't see any tongues hanging out and made sure his wasn't. When the smiling waitress came by, he ordered a half pint and nursed it for the time it took the audience to worm their way out.

"I guess you forgot we had a date for lunch."

He looked up from his contemplation of the glass. "I guess I did." Bright yellow, fake alligator skin shoes. Day-Glo orange tights and brown eyelet-trimmed shorts. He skipped the rest to meet her eyes. "I apologize. I didn't see you."

"I was waiting for you in the park. You said we'd go there today."

"That's true. My fault."

"Don't feel bad. It wasn't set in stone and, after what Kevin said, I wasn't sure you'd want to see me again."

"Kevin?"

"One of the actors. A friend."

Half the men still in the room stared at her, sending him surreptitious glances. They were all in their best casual, smart tourist chinos, loafers and polo shirts. He'd come straight from the site, dusty, gritty, rumpled.

"Isn't that the dancer?" a woman asked, not bothering to keep her voice low. "How odd. You'd never guess looking at her."

"Guess what?" the woman's junk yard dog companion asked.

"That she was even a tiny bit graceful."

"Graceful?" Mike lurched to his feet, leering at the woman. "This lass has more grace in her thumb than you have in your—." He stared at Jakki, reaching to remove her hand from his mouth but she shook her head.

"Let's have a picnic in the park."

He glared at the offending speaker until she was escorted from the building. "Does that happen often?"

"Often enough. Comes with the job." She smiled. "Something about the way I dress."

"You look good to me." His gaze followed the curves of her body, accounting for the green halter top and white fur vest. "What color is that?"

"Mint. Why are you here, Mike?"

"I couldn't very well just not turn up after kissing you, could I?"

"I did wonder about that."

"Good. I've been wondering about that all day."

"Do you mind if we go? I didn't have lunch and I can't think straight when I'm this hungry."

"That could go in my favor," he said.

"No," she said. "It couldn't."

That was clear enough, even for a lovesick mutt. Mike shrugged it off and followed her out. At the door, he offered his arm and she held onto him. Before they reached the bike, he said, "I'd like to take you on a real date."

"That can be arranged. But what have you called these past few nights?"

"Looking after you."

"What kind of date?"

"Dinner. A club. A movie. Some dancing. Take you home."

"Haven't we done all that?"

"And some kissing."

"We've done that too."

"I kissed you. You didn't have a choice."

She didn't deny or confirm. The statement hung in the night sky. His next question remained unasked but they both knew what it was. Only Jakki Hunter knew the answer.

51

eight

The park bench stood far enough from the lamppost for Mike and was well-enough lit for Jakki. The picnic was spread on the bench between them. Mike had eaten his fill. Jakki consumed the rest of the sandwiches and cakes, drank from the bottle of Milwaukee beer.

"I filed a police report on your accident."

She turned her face away, dropped the sandwich onto the bench, wiped her hands on a napkin and folded her arms. He hadn't expected any other response.

"I know you didn't want that. My company has to do it."

"I know."

"There's something else."

She glanced his way but didn't meet his gaze. Mike leaned forward, clasped his hands together, attempted to see her face.

"A medical exam."

"But you said this was okay." She held up her arm, a small, still angry scar peaked from the edge of her sleeve.

"I'm not a doctor, Jakki. If anything happens to you, that will be my fault. I know you said no doctors but I've found someone maybe you won't hate."

"I don't hate doctors. I don't trust them. Any of them."

"What about them don't you trust?"

"They do things."

Mike crouched in front of her, planted his hands on either side of her hips, not touching but close. *Never underestimate a woman's capacity to confound and intrigue.'* His father's sage, married-life quips stopped coming the first time his grown son visited home with a black-eye. Mike couldn't explain. His dad couldn't ask. Mike went home less often. His dad covered for him with his mom. Margery slugged him with a wrench from his toolkit and locked him out.

This was nothing like that. This was different. This girl didn't strike out. She absorbed. Confounded and intrigued. The kind of woman his dad was talking about. All good things for a guy to wrap his head around and never quite get the hang of how her head worked.

"What do you mean, darling' What things?"

"They take you in rooms, put things on your head, make you do funny things."

"That's not going to happen, sweetheart."

"You can't stop it. You'll be part of it."

"Whatever you're afraid of, I won't let anything happen to you. I swear." Even if he asked, she was in no frame of mind to explain. He needed her to agree. He also needed her to trust him, not for the blasted company but for them. What was he thinking? He hardly knew more than he felt good. Like he wanted to wrap her up and keep her, spend hours watching her, be with her, take her places. See what she wore every day. "I'm sorry this has happened to you. But I'm glad we've met. I'm glad I know you."

"I told you I'm a celebrity."

"You did. Since you were fourteen."

"I couldn't go anywhere. I don't know how they found out but I couldn't get away. It was like being in a cage, everyone watching, waiting for me to perform some wild trick, do all the crazy things they imagined I had done to make my parents so mad."

"Is that why you're in this play?"

"It's the only thing I'm good at."

Refuting that statement was an argument to nowhere. He stuck to the matter. "I didn't want to do this but once I thought about it—."

53

She pulled away but he stopped her.

"I can't even remember my own name when I'm around you." Off topic. Off everything that made any sense. "All I know for sure is I want to be around you. Five years ago, I was hit by a car and left for dead. No one saw the car. If not for the company and my insurance, I'd be dead. This guy isn't worth it. Don't protect him."

"I'm not."

"Do you want him to go around thinking he can treat people like that? What if the next time, he kills the girl?"

"That won't happen. He won't do anything like that again."

"How do you know?"

"I know."

The set of her jaw, the flare in her eyes stopped him from pursuing the matter.

"I'm glad someone knows something," he said, straightening his legs, slow and easy into an upright position. "I sure don't know much about you and from what I *do* know, it's unlikely you want me to know anything more."

"You saw what happened."

"Hey, I'm not that guy. Not even remotely that kind of guy."

"Maybe not but I'm that kind of girl. Sooner or later, I get tossed out like so much garbage."

"Not with me."

"I know you believe that, Mike."

"I would never do anything like that."

"Not now but one day, you'll get tired of me, my quirks. Gavin is a really nice guy too. One morning, bang, he's had enough and I'm on the ground at your feet. It'll happen. It always does."

"No, Jakki, that's not who I am."

"I know you won't want to." She looked everywhere but at him, refused to meet his steady gaze. "No one wants to at first."

"You're making some pretty sweeping assumptions about me, lady." He leaned down, smiling into her wide-eyed stare.

"I'm damned sure you don't know me any better than I know you so let's give each other a break." He extended his hand and helped her to her feet. "I'm pretty sure I know a doctor who's not a threat – at least not as far as I could see based on the little I know about you. If you won't see her, I'll explain to my company. That won't stop them from harassing you. But," he said, gathering up the remains of the picnic, "that will not, will *not* mean I won't be coming around to take you places and wanting to kiss you, whatever you do about kissing me. Up to you."

"That's an ultimatum." She lifted her gaze to meet him half way, slid forward on the bench.

"No, lady, it is not. You are stuck with me, whatever your choice about this doctor. And don't bother giving me any bull about not wanting me around. We both know you can't lie."

"I'll sue your company for harassment."

"Go ahead. They've got good lawyers and plenty of them."

"I have a good lawyer."

"Great. The lawyers will be having just about as much fun as I will." He grinned and swooped down to kiss her, wrapped her up in his big arms. Not a cold response. A slight yield, no full surrender yet. The dog was making progress. *Maybe.* A little sorrowful eye contact, nudging her with his shaggy head.

He hugged her tight, dancing the two-step like they had at the church, moved his paw to press her closer. Big, hot, dusty, gritty all around this graceful, delicate, fragile anomaly.

"How can you dance in these crazy shoes?"

"One step at a time."

nine

Music floated on icy air from one of the grand stone houses on St. Andrews Square around the park. The blasted pipes just a faint undercurrent from the hawkers on Princes Street. Their dance ended on a shrug, his one-sided smile and her sigh. Leaving the remains of the picnic for the vagabonds of the Fringe, they walked, arm in arm, out of the park toward the Firth. Not talking.

He had her promise to come with him to see Sula Kanipataraja, GP.

She had his promise to stay with her through the appointment.

Jimmy could handle the supervision on the site while he was gone. He wasn't as confident that Ferguson would let him get on with the report without interference.

He wanted to take her to his place but knew better than to mention it. If she wanted to see where he lived, she'd tell him they were going there. He was sure she'd appreciate the view. He didn't have to worry about any mess. He was never home long enough to do any damage.

When they reached a footbridge, he put his arm around her shoulders. She kept her arms at her sides, tucked in at the elbows. He felt about fifteen, but it wasn't a bad feeling, being half his age, hanging out with a girl he couldn't figure, who didn't make him feel like an idiot every time he spoke.

In the middle of the footbridge, they stopped to look down at the water. Tourists walked all around them, quiet, tired, bewildered, intoxicated. Mike lowered his arm and leaned over the railing.

"Don't!"

He pulled back, watching Jakki over his shoulder. Her hands gripped the railing, like steel. She stared at some distant spot. He straightened his back and turned to face her. "Water's cold tonight."

"Too cold." Her knuckles turned white. "I can't look. If I look, if I look…"

"Let's keep walking."

She nodded, still gripping the rail. Mike clasped her left hand, pried one finger away at a time, sliding his hand underneath each finger in turn to replace the cold, white rail. Once loosened, she slipped one arm through his, loosened her right hand and gripped his. When they reached the other side of the bridge, in time to watch a midnight juggling act, she sagged a little, rested on one tortured foot, then the other. Mike picked her up and set her down on a wall, turned his back to watch the act.

After a moment, she dropped her arms around his neck and leaned forward so his head rested against her breasts. He almost choked but kept his cool. Her legs wrapped around his waist and he brought them close with his arms hooked under her knees, clasping his hands over his belly. Jakki didn't object any more than he objected to her arms around him. He felt so good. He wanted to turn around and kiss her, distract her from the show, focus on him but there was a good reason to give her the initiative and all the opportunities for advance.

Two of the ugliest shoes he'd ever seen were on two of the loveliest legs he'd ever held around him. If he turned and pulled her forward he'd have a perfect moment before she got away. And he wanted that moment. He wanted to nestle and confirm but that wasn't going to happen. He dropped his chin onto her crossed wrists, tempted to kiss her fingers.

Holding back came naturally. Not something he did especially for this girl. Cautious. Been burned, caught, twisted up and spit out enough not to make mistakes in reading signals. This girl's signals were too confusing to be sure he read right. On one level, she said 'go' and, on another, a big 'stop' loomed in front of him. He was going with the flow, following as it went. Not offering. Not regretting or resisting. Just lazy and mellow.

The juggler tossed his batons to spectators in the street, picking the pretty girls. Though Mike's girl was the prettiest, the batons never came close. Other girls were disappointed but Jakki sighed in relief. She pressed her cheek against his temple. "He's been after me for weeks to be in his act."

He turned his head to ask a question and she kissed him. A peck and she was gone.

"Thanks, Mike."

"What for?"

"For running defense." Her legs swung forward and back.

"My pleasure."

The juggler worked his recruits to the audience's delight, tricking them and making them clumsy for the amusement of the crowd. Their friends enjoyed their humiliation as much as the strangers. Anyone not concentrating on the action would think the juggler was a creep for tormenting the innocents. Mike had lost his grip for a moment but, with two Fringe experiences under his tool belt, he caught the juggler's signals to his shills.

Jakki had kissed him, that kept sneaking into focus. Sweet. Promising. *Hold on, Mike. There's more. A lot more.* He rubbed his chin on her wrist and raised his head.

"Let's go."

"Okay. Where to now?" Once they were on the edge of the crowd, she took his hand and walked back toward the bridge.

"Will you let me take you out tomorrow night? After your performance, on a date?"

"I guess."

Not even close to the silly enthusiasm he felt. Nowhere near his anticipation but *I guess* amounted to agreement and he went with that. *Let it happen. Whatever it is.*

"The appointment I made for you to see this doctor?"

"When?"

"I'll pick you up at eleven. The doctor promised she'd make it quick and painless."

"You'll be there?"

"Yes."

"Okay."

Still laughing, he pushed his motorbike into the alleyway by his building. *Yeah. Pretty much. Maybe.* If he'd taken one step at a time with Margery, he'd have found out sooner why he needed to run like hell before she got her hooks in him. But no, *if* he'd been smart then, he wouldn't be here in Edinburgh, hiding out and dancing in the park with the progeny of faeries.

Jimmy laughed at him like he wore the choke chain he felt around his neck. Not a word when the rental car company called back to confirm the pick-up at five:PM. Not a word when Mike made a reservation at the East Asian restaurant on Thistle. The Scotsman's stoicism cracked again when Mike phoned for tourist information on ballroom dance venues but he split open like a demolition ball hitting a brick wall at the sight of Mike shaving again at ten:fifteen when he'd come in at seven:AM cut as close as a bridegroom.

"Bad ain't the word for how you've got it, Mickey."

"Feels good to me, Jimmy." He was out the door, loosening the choke chain by giving in to the pull. As he got closer to her house in Musselburgh, he wasn't feeling any restraint on his heart muscle. He roared into the narrow street with its side-by-side-by-side houses and rail fences, rolled the bike up the walk and rang the bell.

When someone inside was roused enough to shuffle to the door, Mike caught a glimpse of a bleared eye and stubble, dingy skin and low-hanging denims.

"Yeah?" Not a Scotsman. Not American either.

"I'm here to pick up Jakki."

"Yeah? You must have the wrong house."

"Excuse me?" Should have said *Pardon*. The guy was spoiling for a fight. Mike recognized him from the play, one of the main characters, in your face type, ready to take on lesser beings, but no one his match.

"Why? What have you done?"

Picking him up by the front of his t-shirt was in order but the cloth sagged and gave no leverage. Mike walked him into the narrow hallway with the guy spluttering and indignant. That blasted twinge caught Mike on his left side or he'd have put Mr. Yeah through the door into the front room with one sharp shove.

"Where's Jakki?"

"I told you. There's no one here by that name. Piss off." Yeah pulled at Mike's fist.

"She lives here. Either you tell me where, which room or I put you through that wall."

"What's your problem?"

Good question. Ratcheting down, something about the guy. Something about the girl. "Just tell me." Calmer. Not scared she was sleeping with Yeah. *Not much.* Mike shook his head, laughed, short, sharp.

"Put him down, Mike."

His fist opened and he swung toward the back of the house. Yeah stumbled back, rubbing his chest.

"We don't let assholes like you anywhere near her so just get out," Yeah said, taking a stand to the side, out of Mike's range.

"Are you ready, darlin'?"

"She's not going anywhere with you, asshole."

"I'll be back in time to go to the theater with you," Jakki told Yeah as she walked past both men.

Mike turned on his heel and followed the orange heels and tight, hot pink jersey dress. She had already pulled the overalls from the cargo holder before Yeah got to the front door.

"You're going with him?"

"Seems so," Mike said, zipping up the front for her, keeping his eyes on her face.

"Don't come crying, like all the other times," Yeah sneered. "We're all tired of your whining."

Jakki glanced at Mike, said nothing as she swung her leg over the saddle.

Mike winced a little when he settled and revved the engine. What was he thinking, picking fights with guys half his size? Any guy no matter what size. Not like him. Yeah hadn't done a thing, just there, living with her. Protecting her from guys like him and just as quick to brush her off when she made a choice he didn't like.

Control. That was it. Control. Yeah wanted it. He wanted it. She wasn't letting it happen. *Simple. Maybe.*

ten

The office on Union Street had bright painted doors and window frames. The colors jumped out from the gray stone, desperate to be seen in the drab morning haze. Jakki hung back as they crossed the pavement and stood behind him when he opened the door. *Fear. Control.*

Mike stepped across the threshold and held the door open for her but made no other attempt to force her to enter. He didn't look at her or make any comment or gesture. He waited. Someone walked out past him but he didn't notice until the woman thanked him for holding the door and pushed between Jakki and the entry way.

Jakki stepped back to let the woman pass. Mike was tempted to grab her arm to keep her from making an escape but she stayed, moved forward, hovered and crossed the threshold into the foyer.

At the reception desk, Mike checked in. Jakki occupied an armchair in a corner of the waiting room, searching the paisley-patterned carpet, her hands clasped tight at her knees. He sat in the chair nearest her, covering her hands with his big paw. She trembled like a puppy. With his free hand, he stroked her cheek but she was non-responsive.

When the receptionist called her name, Mike stood. Jakki looked up. He offered his hand and she clasped it. A slight pull. Resistance. He loosened his grip and she tightened hers, rose to her feet. The clinic nurse told him he could stay in the waiting room.

"I want him to come in."

"That's not appropriate, Miss Hunter. Mr. Argent is an employee of the construction company," the nurse said.

"I know that."

"The examination won't take long. Mr. Argent will be in the next room," Dr. Kanipataraja assured her, greeting Mike with a nod.

"So will I," Jakki replied. When his doctor scoffed in protest, Jakki turned on her heel. "I won't stay here, Mike. No examination."

"Mr. Argent, will you explain your position to Miss Hunter. It is most irregular for a company employee to be present in such cases. If you stay, this may hinder Miss Hunter's case against the driver of the vehicle."

"I have no case against him. I'm only here because Mike asked me. He stays or I go."

"I'll stay out of your way, Dr. Kanipataraja," he said, leaning against the wall. "I won't listen or watch—."

"You must!"

Mike caught Jakki's hand and squeezed to quell her panic. "I will. I'm here for you."

"I'll have to put this in my report, Mr. Argent. I have no idea what your company will say about this."

"That won't be a problem, Doctor. Pretend I don't exist."

Dr. Kanipataraja rolled her eyes on a sigh and pointed to a chair for Jakki. The examination began with a few questions, innocent questions that became more specific, invasive and insinuating. Through them, Jakki remained unperturbed.

"And the driver of this vehicle was a friend of yours by the name of Gavin Andrews?"

Jakki gave no response.

'This is a matter of record, Miss Hunter. His car and license number have been confirmed by the police."

"What do you want me to say?"

"Was Mr. Gavin Andrews driving the car from which you were thrown?"

"I wasn't thrown."

"Did you jump?"

"Yes, I jumped."

"Was Mr. Andrews driving the car from which you jumped?"

"Yes."

Mike pulled his eyebrows down in a deep frown. She lied for Andrews and he wanted to know why. The doctor made some comment he didn't hear and began the physical exam.

Did she love the jerk enough to lie to protect him? Did she still love him? What the hell did he care about that? It wasn't like he was in love with her. She could be as crazy as she wanted with any guy, for any guy.

It didn't mean anything to him. He was the next in line. Panting and slavering but what red-blooded guy wouldn't? She was with him, liked him, maybe even felt a twinge when he touched her. He'd find out for sure. Later. And his intentions were not honorable.

Dr. Kanipataraja was back at her desk, writing at top speed. Jakki twisted in her chair, swung her leg, dangled her orange stilt from her toes.

"You did a good job, Mr. Argent."

"Pardon?"

"Your first aid intervention. Good work."

"Basic medic stuff. First Responder training."

Kanipataraja hummed an impatient agreement and said, "You've reported no underlying health issues, Miss Hunter, but without your full medical history, I'm limited to what I can ascertain for any long term affects. If you have your GP send those—."

"No. That's impossible."

"This is all entirely confidential, I assure you. There is no reason for you to worry."

"No one will ever see them."

Both Kanipataraja and Mike studied her a moment.

"I don't have to explain to you or anyone," Jakki said, standing. "If you're finished, I have a performance this evening." She reached the door and passed the nurse before Mike pushed up from the chair.

"The report will be sent to Peter Ferguson within a week," Sula Kanipataraja said to his back.

He acknowledged the assurance with a nod and a hasty "thanks" before he caught up to Jakki at the street door. "I'll take you to the theater."

"I'm going home. I can take care of myself."

"Okay. I'll get you home." When she shrugged, he said, "We have a date tonight."

"So you said."

"I don't say, I ask. If you're going to stand me up, I'd appreciate advanced warning."

"Why would I do that? I have a new outfit."

Relief came nowhere near describing the leap in his chest. Nothing in all his experience compared. *Deep trouble.* Not even close to the heights he'd reached. *New outfit?* Had to be beyond bizarre.

"I'll look forward to seeing it." Lame but he couldn't fall on his knees in the middle of Union Street and throw his arms around her legs though that was what he wanted to do.

"I thought you might," she said with a coy swing of her hips.

Right then and there he couldn't move for the shock of seeing her, with him, somewhere, anywhere, there on Union Street, on the back of his bike, in his bed. She got to him. In every way it was possible for a woman to bring a man begging, she did it. Her long bare legs straddled his bike. Her thighs slid around his hips. He struggled to stay calm when his only thought was to plunge. Bury his whole being in all her quirks and breathe fire.

That was good. Real good. The best he'd felt in years and at the same time he saw her in bed with Yeah and Kevin and half a dozen other guys who wanted her as bad as he did. He wanted an exclusive.

At her house, she came off his bike and waved. He rode to the end of the street and forced his brain to work on solving some other problem before he risked going back to the Princes Street construction site all worked up like a kid.

Jimmy gave him a quick once over and a grin before he had stowed his jacket but there were no physical signs of what was going on in his head. He was ripe to burst when he got back to his flat in the rental car.

Another shave, shower, a change of clothes took the edge of the chokehold, churned up something new. That heart thumping anticipation he had lost, buried years ago.

So far, she surprised him but never disappointed. He was spruced up and ready for his first date in six years. He was in plenty of time to get to the theater and find a place to park that he didn't have to worry about the car sliding down the hill. He checked the state of his appearance in the rearview mirror one more time and strolled up the hill. The girl at the box office recognized him and was all smiles when he came through the door in suit, dress shirt, tie and shiny shoes.

"I know all about you," she whispered as she handed over his ticket and change.

"I doubt it," he laughed in return.

"Jakki told me."

He raised an eyebrow and leaned a little closer. "What, exactly?"

"That you're taking her on a date."

"Does that surprise you?"

"No, but I'd be lying if I said I wasn't jealous. The lads I know don't know what a date is."

Mike winked and walked into the theater, feeling so good, he was almost dancing. She talked about him. Seemed she didn't say anything bad, no complaints, not laughing behind his back.

He sat at the same table as on previous nights. The waitress/usherette brought him the drink he had ordered on other nights. The audience was as small as before. No repeaters other than him. Same talking and laughing. Same posturing and self-importance. Same setting the ever-present, always-connected, never-touching smartphone to silent vibrating.

The few smiles from the waitress and the ticket clerk cheered him up but he kept his eyes on his drink, traced his fingers down the glass through the cold sweat, grateful when the lights dimmed.

The actress he had seen the first night came on the stage in Jakki's place. The kick of disappointment hit him in his gut but he held it together through the first scenes. Yeah was on stage, top form, holding his own at the same time Mike was losing his.

eleven

The sound wasn't part of the performance but the actors went on as if they hadn't heard it, though each of them registered an acknowledgement. Imperceptible to most of the audience. All part of the experimental genre experience.

Mike leapt onto the stage and was exiting upstage left when he heard a man's voice, indistinct against the dismal drone of pipes from every direction.

Whoever the man was didn't have his hands on Jakki, wasn't even close but the look in her eyes was enough for Mike.

"Unless you want to deal with me, I suggest you leave the way you came in."

There were no sounds of alarm from the stage, or the audience, but he kept his voice low. He rolled his eyes. *Damn avant garde. They'd think a murder was all part of the act.*

"You'd be the one she's latched onto after me, that right, laddie?"

"I have no idea what you're talking about, but I'm not a lad and you're causing a disturbance. Leave or I'll toss you out." Confident he looked like he could do that easily, Mike stepped forward.

"Any disturbance I make would be an improvement on what this lot get up to."

The intruder's voice rose, strident, stressed and grating on Mike's nerves. Just low enough to be male but whiny and snide. Mike took another step and the man backed away from Jakki.

"You know she's a loon. She'll flip out on you in a bloody flash, laddie."

"Insulting Miss——." He thought better of giving her name to anyone. She'd never told him, why should she have it blundered out to a creep? "—A lady is no way to get my attention." He took a final step and, from the way the guy reacted, he figured he didn't need to raise a finger. "The door's right there, bud. Out you go."

"I'm not done with you, Jakki. The next time you talk to the damn police, tell them what you did."

Mike yanked the door open and waved the guy out. He turned his back on the door and leaned against it.

"You know some choice examples of assholes, darlin'."

"He didn't start out that way."

"Bull. I can read a jerk a mile away."

"Thank you for coming down."

"No problem. You ready to go?"

"The performance isn't over."

"You're not on stage so——."

"I'm still part of the show and besides I'm not wearing this."

"I wondered why you weren't performing tonight. I thought you'd changed your mind about our date."

"I like to give Rache a chance to perform."

"Rache?"

"My understudy. Just in case."

Mike studied her a moment. "Are you okay? That jerk is a nasty customer."

"I'm used to that."

"So you've said before. What's the attraction?" He laughed. "I know why they're attracted to you. Why do *you* pick them?"

She didn't answer. She might never answer that question. He knew the answer. It was the same answer he'd never cop to, except in the darkest hour of the night, when there was no way to escape it, when all the curtains were wide open and all the lies were disproved and the honest truth couldn't be denied. The same answer had kept him crawling back to Margery. *What else was there for him? What else could he expect?*

"My ex-wife used to make me sleep in my car." Lord help him, he couldn't hold that back anymore, not from this girl. She had quirks. He had shame, humiliation, emasculation in triple digits. "What else have you got to do before we go?"

"I need to watch the rest of the performance so I can give Rache some pointers, she's studying for college."

Another surprise. "You teach?"

"She's on work experience. We can get out to the front this way." He followed down a narrow hallway that opened onto the back of the theater, near his table. His drink was gone. Keeping quiet for a big construction worker was a sure recipe for calamity and his attempt to pull a chair out for his date finished in a clatter of demolition proportions.

His disheartened sink into his chair won him a pat on the wrist. Mike took the gesture of patronizing forgiveness as an invitation and clasped her hand, rewarded by the feel of her fingers curling into his heavy paw. Soft. Sweet as a baby's hand. Trusting. He wasn't thinking about what the whiner said. He wasn't thinking about Yeah even though he was on stage. He wasn't thinking about any other guy at her house. *Not much.*

He was looking at their hands, joined together on the table, in the open, simple and warm. Her flesh all soft and his hard and calloused. He was thinking about how he'd feel with all of her curling around him. He was thinking about raspberries and blueberries, following all the swirls with his mouth, tracing the chocolate swathe with his tongue, dipping into her secrets like a kid in a candy shop, sampling all the sweetest things.

A man could die from the sugar overdose if he wasn't dining in moderation. Who cared about surviving a trip on the Good Ship Lollipop?

But he wasn't even on the gangway. He was on the dock, lost his sea legs a long time ago, at least for voyages like this one had to be. Why wasn't he thinking short pleasure cruise, a little speedboat and quick trip around the lagoon? Why was he thinking about global circumnavigation, longitude and latitude, tropics, deserts, beaches, mountains, valleys, caves—caves and underwater caverns, plains, rough seas, bays and fast flowing rivers into estuaries?

A drink appeared beside his unoccupied hand. He looked up but the waitress was gone. Yeah gave his mighty soliloquy and Rache danced by herself in the corner. A man sat beside Jakki but Mike hadn't seen him arrive either. The two of them were whispering in each other's ear, inaudible to everyone else, and Mike wanted to push him to the floor for distracting his date.

She wasn't thinking about him or any of the places he wanted to take her with his lovemaking. She held his hand but she was engaged in conversation with someone else. How he felt was juvenile—he owned up to that—but with all he'd seen for himself and heard from other guys, the uncertainty mounted to about the same intensity his desire to mount her had reached.

Uncertainty and desire collided.

He clasped the drink and downed it in one swallow, loosened his grip on his date and pushed back his chair noiselessly. Her hand convulsed on his for a moment and when he stood, she lifted her face, met his gaze.

"Are you coming back?" It wasn't the question, but the look in her eyes when she asked it.

"Darlin', we have a date."

He could live on next to nothing and had for a long time, but her smile went straight to his gut. If he was scared of what she could do to him before, seeing that look and watching her light up brought it home like a torpedo mid-ship. He was dead in the water, no life jacket, sinking like the U.S.S. Liberty.

Maybe he was kidding himself. Maybe he saw what he wanted to see. Maybe all the other men she'd known had been blown out of the water by that same look. Maybe it was all an act to keep him and all the others on side until she dropped them but it didn't feel like that. He'd learned from some of the best heartbreakers and this didn't get close to the anxiety those women could generate with a look.

Yes, he was scared but when it came down to it, he was scared this wasn't going to sink. He was scared this was going to float and what would he do when his job came to an end and her tour was over and where would they decide to live?

He was thinking permanent. Forever. And they hadn't been on a first date and he'd never seen her naked or first thing in the morning. He didn't care.

The men's room stank as usual. One guy was holding himself up by butting his head on the wall above the urinal. Mike turned on his heel. He didn't want any drunk using his good suit for a hand towel.

The performance neared the end and Jakki was still in conversation with the other man. Mike, too agitated to be sure of keeping quiet, stood at the end of the bar and waved the offer of a drink away.

Jakki's head was bowed, listening, responding, debating, agreeing, disagreeing. All under her breath. She used both her hands, since he wasn't there to claim one of them as his own possession, to illustrate and emphasize. Her hands were lithe, graceful, quick. He wanted to feel them on his body. She hadn't made any venture to explore him the way he had when he fixed her arm. Was she even remotely interested? She had kissed him once. Spontaneous. Once. Was that the most she offered?

There was only one way to know. If he wanted more, he had to expect more. *If you don't ask, you don't get.*

She was lively with the other man. She was fragile with him. Those were the two sides Mike saw the most often. And the cold, aloof side. The self-protection, the scared little girl, the damaged woman—he had met them all. Not one of them hinted at the fire he felt.

He observed for a little while more, until end of the show. The man left and Jakki was on her own for a moment. She remained quiet, her hands on the table, still and idle. She didn't look around. She didn't search for him. He wondered what she expected. Perhaps exactly what had happened to her before. Why, he wondered, did all the other men blame her? What had they expected? The same as he expected. All that beauty waiting for the only man who made the trip to understand her?

Mike stood up straight. *Why not?*

"Has anyone taken this seat?"

"No."

twelve

When he landed in the seat he had vacated, Jakki faced him square on. "I have to talk to Rache for a little while. Do you want to wait here or shall I meet you outside?"

"I'm happy here."

The understudy dropped into the seat the man had left and sighed so heavily she shook the table. "Ter said you wanted to talk to me." Rache cast a long look at Mike and cocked her head.

"I want to go over a few points with you."

"I was awful. I know. I could feel it." She gave Mike a flirtatious smile, a little pout for his sympathy. He returned a weak smile, kept his attention focused on his date, willing her to move on with the feedback so he could be alone with her for the rest of the night.

"First, you need to judge your own performances with less emotion and self-doubt. Your performance was good, Rache. The audience was with you for most of the time when they were supposed to be. When the action was on the other actors, you relinquished their attention."

"I thought that's what I was supposed to do. Kevin wouldn't have been very happy if I carried on dancing like some crazy woman when he was performing his bit."

The understudy's blatant dig at her mentor went unchallenged. His girl wasn't popular with her fellow actors but she didn't court them either.

"That isn't what I'm saying," Jakki continued. "You are supposed to relinquish the audience's attention, but you also lost your own focus."

"I don't think so. I was doing just what you told me."

"You were disengaged, Rache. You were going through the motions."

The girl sat for a moment, let out a deep breath. "Is that all?"

"For now," Jakki replied.

"I guess you want to get out of here with your hot date again." She jumped from the chair and pirouetted across the floor. "I don't zone-out as bad as some." She was gone before Jakki responded.

"Nice girl," Mike said. "She'll go far." He clasped Jakki's hand and stood up. "Ready to go?"

"I want to change."

"You look fine to me."

"Thank you but these are my working clothes."

He looked her over from head to foot and couldn't say there was any difference from what she had worn on any other evening before or after the performance. Totally edible as far as the junk yard dog could see. What about her made him think of himself in a junk yard or lost at sea? It had to be something that set him off balance. Still to be revealed. "From where I'm standing, you're perfect."

"Next to you, I'm a ragdoll," she said, taking his hand and leading the way backstage and down to the lower dressing rooms. She left him to wait in the erstwhile green room where Yeah—otherwise known as Kevin—and Jakki's confidante were talking. The confidante turned his eyes on Mike, looked him up and down as if he was something nasty tracked in on the bottom of Jakki's shoes.

"Are you the medic?"

"I suppose I am."

"You should have taken her to Casualty. That scar's going to be ugly."

"Nothing to do with me."

"Right." The confidante gave him a final sneer and turned his back. "Where does she find these assholes?"

Kevin shrugged. "I'm not picking up the pieces any more. That's for certain."

The confidante glared at the actor, rolled his eyes and walked away.

Mike stared at the clock. The reservation at the restaurant gave them another twenty minutes. He'd timed it loose to give her leeway but he hadn't reckoned on as many delays as this. What if she doesn't like Far Eastern cuisine. Too late. Should have asked.

Behind him, Kevin whistled, said something under his breath.

"I'm ready, Mike."

Before he turned, he prepared himself for whatever surprise her anxious tone warned him of, but he needn't have. "You look pretty." How lame was that? But she did. Pale pink evening dress. Stockings. Sheer enough to be as sexy as bare. The stilettos were pink silk. Tiny gold earrings. Pretty and feminine. Not at all what he anticipated. He took a moment to register the letdown. On any other girl, the outfit would have been perfect. On her, for him, it was tame.

"Thank you." She swept a black velvet cape around her shoulders and pulled the hood over her hair—*and* the narrow pink bow over her ear.

She preceded him up the stairs. Down the back of her stockings was a pattern. He let her get a few steps ahead and grinned. *That's more like it.* Skulls and cross bones led his eyes up her long, long legs to the delicate voile hem of her dress. Beyond that barrier he let his imagination play around for a while but he kept his hungry fingers to himself.

In the theater, she waved at the box office clerk who grinned back and winked at Mike. At least he had one friend in the company. The waitress/usherette watched him leave and gave the box office girl a nod. Seems he and Jakki had a few allies.

His date walked ahead of him, expecting him to follow. That panting junk yard dog was right back in the game, still wondering what it was about this girl that had him tied up and wanting any scraps she tossed his way. Whatever it was, it woke him up, kept him wondering, challenged everything he thought he knew about women. He wasn't sure he wanted more than a few good times with Jakki Hunter but finding that out was something to look forward to.

At the makeshift theater's entrance, Jakki waited for him to open the door for her, took his arm when he came out and looked up and down the hill.

"We'll have to walk a bit."

"Where did you park your bike?"

"No bike tonight." He should have hired a chauffeur, a limo, give himself plenty of opportunity to enjoy her company, plenty of time to work his charm on her defenses or whatever the barrier was she raised between her and her men friends. "I rented a car for the occasion. So you didn't have to fight with my overalls, nice as it is to lend a hand in that procedure."

She gave him a full smile and squeezed his arm, her breasts pressed against his bicep. He flexed the muscle and she pulled away but not before he caught a look of bewilderment, surprise and maybe a little secret pleasure. He held her hand on his forearm and walked down the hill. She held tight and he grabbed her around the waist a few times to keep her from tumbling but that was a pleasure too.

When they reached level ground, he turned toward her, slipping his arms around her waist. She neither resisted nor surrendered, keeping her arms at her sides, looking into his eyes.

"Let's get this straight, Miss Hunter. I asked you on a date. You accepted. Since it's my date and invitation, it's my check. No splitting the bill, agreed?" Before she spoke, he went on, "No strings. No expectations. I'm happy with the fact you said yes. Nothing else has to happen…unless you want it. Okay with you?"

"Is that a promise, Mr. Argent?"

"Scout's honor. I won't promise not to try. You are the prettiest, most tantalizing, mysterious woman I've known since I was fifteen. I'd be lying if I said I didn't want to make love to you. But if it's no for you, I'll back off—until the next time."

"I don't want to mislead you, Mr. Argent. I like being with you. You're a good person and I wouldn't have accepted this date if I didn't feel comfortable. But it is always no with me and I don't anticipate that changing. I really don't want to hurt you but if you persist in trying to seduce me, you will be disappointed."

"I'll take that chance," he said, pulling her closer to him, "just for the privilege of being the guy who helps you walk in those crazy shoes."

"You are the best so far," she said, looking beyond him, behind him, beside him—anywhere but at him.

"As a walking stick."

"Yes."

Mike heard the relief in her voice and smiled as he gave her a quick hug. This girl had more commitment issues than the hardest player he'd ever known. He thought about making promises, commitments and challenges to be the best at a lot more. Instead he said, "Good to know," and walked her to the compact rented car.

"This is nice of you."

"Forethought isn't one of my strongest characteristics. By the time I got the idea of a driver and limo, it was too late."

"I've ridden in a limo."

Her tone and expression told him she was lucky to be alive to tell the tale. Mike opened the door at the kerb, and held her hand while she maneuvered her legs and hips into the front seat. He blocked images of those hips swaying to the Swing rhythm in his head. No good to even try. He felt her soft and warm right where it did him the most good and took a moment, outside the car to ratchet down.

When he folded himself into the seat and gripped the wheel, he was back in control but not for long. She touched his thigh. He almost drove onto the sidewalk and into a lone piper.

"Okay?"

"Sorry. Not used to driving enclosed." That was a lie but she bought it. No further mishaps prevented their arrival at the restaurant. The maître'd walked them through the dining room to a booth and took Jakki's cape. When she turned, her skirt swirled, revealing the tops of her stockings and the red lace of her garters.

Mike ran his fingers around the inside of his choke chain passing for a shirt collar. Ratcheting down was getting to be a permanent condition, brought on by deliberate provocation. Or in complete innocence. Mike had no idea.

"I don't know anything about this food," she said after reading and re-reading the items on the menu.

"Mild, spicy or hot?"

"Spicy."

"Meat, poultry, fish or vegetarian?"

"Any or all."

He ordered crab, chicken and beef according to her preferences, lychee cocktails and water with mint and lime slices.

When the appetizers arrived, he served her half and waited for her to taste them before he devoured what remained on the plate.

"How long have you been in the theater?" he asked while they waited for the rest of the meal.

"Not long."

Unresponsive. "I've never had much interest in plays. Seen a few of the classics, but not since high school."

"What do you like?"

Better. She didn't mind talking about him, asking him questions. Once in a while she let her guard down with something about her. Like riding in limos. He had no trouble imagining what a guy could get up to in a limo with a beautiful, long-legged woman. He had no trouble figuring out what she wouldn't like about being trapped in a limo with such a guy.

"When I can't sleep, I watch films or read."

"What keeps you awake, Mike?"

He had opened that door. Had wanted to get it out like he'd wanted to tell her about how Margery had treated him in the last year of their marriage. If he was going to have anything with this girl, she had to have some warning.

"Pain."

thirteen

She nodded and pushed her food around her plate for a moment. He figured she was asking herself if she wanted to be hooked up with a decrepit guy or know any more about him. She plucked up a piece of chicken with her chopsticks and opened her mouth. Pretty mouth. Perfect for kissing. She sucked the chicken in. He swallowed hard, that damn choke chain. No amount of ratcheting was going to work on what he was thinking.

"What kind of pain?"

She had asked. He took a moment to savor that small spark of triumph. "Job hazard."

"What kind of hazard?"

"The hit and run driver road construction kind."

"The one you mentioned. Bad?"

"Bad enough." Although he had opened the gates on this conversation, he did not want to have it and he did not want her sympathy. Somehow, her remembering anything he said was enough.

"I guess that explains why you were so insistent about the police report."

"That would be part of it. I'm not a big fan of people who think they have a right to break the law because they don't get caught. The driver who took me for a ride on his rear bumper, then killed four kids who were coming home from a football game. I was the lucky one that night."

"Was he caught?"

"He left me for dead, killed the kids, lost control of his vehicle and escaped justice by dying at the bottom of a cliff. Can't say I wasn't glad he was dead. One less drunken pinhead on the road."

"Mike?"

"What?" He had a gut feeling before she asked but he kept his mouth shut.

"Gavin asked me to drop the charges."

"I figured he would."

"He'll lose his job."

"And?"

"I don't want that."

He wanted anything but the conversation that was spoiling his first date with this girl. "There's nothing I can do. You didn't file the report. I did. All you had to do was have a medical exam to exonerate my company and my first aid treatment. My company won't let this go. I won't let this go."

"But it can't be that important to you."

"I know what I saw. Jimmy and a few of the other crew members saw the same thing. No one deserves to be treated that way and if you're thinking of lying for him," he did not want to say it but he did, "we're done." He folded his napkin on the table.

"Mike, please try to understand."

"I don't want to understand. I want to have a meal, go dancing and have a pleasant conversation with a beautiful woman. I do not want to be talking about a spoiled brat who can't control his temper but thinks everyone else should for his sake. If your boyfriend was here, I'd show him what I think of him for even asking you to do that."

"You won't even consider—."

"No."

"But why?"

"For you. And for the next girl who might make him mad. You could have been killed. The next girl may not be as lucky. Can I make it any plainer than that?"

"Not really."

"Good. Finish your meal." He wasn't hungry anymore but he ate, in silence, watching her eat, thinking how he wanted to get his hands on whoever it was who made her think it was okay to treat her like that.

She ate her meal, looking everywhere in the dining area except at him. That made him mad. The longer he was silent, the more certain he was that he was making a big mistake. When the waiter neared the table, Mike asked for the desert menu. He ordered two and watched her eat the biggest portions of both. As she finished, he paid the tab and was relieved she didn't argue.

The waiter brought her cape and Mike held it open for her, draping it over her shoulders, holding his hands steady as he smoothed the velvet over her, surprised when she nudged her head against his jaw, more surprised when she lifted her chin and offered her lips to be kissed.

He obliged. If he hadn't taken full control of himself, he would have made love to her on the table, regardless of the other patrons. He was tired of flaring only to cool off immediately.

She took his hand and started toward the door. He followed like a little boy. Outside, she leaned into him with a heavy sigh, dropping her head on his shoulder as they walked through the crowd of Festival tourists and the hawkers who took advantage of them.

"What made you come here, darlin'?"

"The Fringe is one of those things you have to do, part of the ritual. Why are you here?"

"Job related."

"Is that the only reason?"

"Pretty much." He knew better. She had already read him. "The job came up. I wanted a change of scene, clear my head."

"To get away from bad memories."

"Never works quite the way I think it will." He searched his pockets for the car key, unlocked the doors. Before she turned away to get in, he caught her in his arms. "I'm loco about you."

"Don't be."

"Too late. Can't stop it."

"I like you too."

"Good to know." People walked past, gave him condescending glances, smirking smiles. All the things he hated about strangers who thought they knew what's going on. He straightened his back and pressed his chin on the top of her head, rubbing a little to feel her short hair tickling him. "I wasn't going to do this, not again. Not after getting flayed alive the last time."

She pulled her head away and stared at him sideways. "Don't."

"Too late," he laughed. "I'm hooked."

"I'm sorry."

"It feels good."

"That won't last."

"So you've told me once or twice before." He held her, loosening his grip when she pulled away. "I want to meet your parents."

"Why?"

"They made you, didn't they? They must be pretty special people."

She yanked away and spun on her stiletto, striding on long legs, picking up speed and, when her shoes failed her, she ripped them off and threw them at his head. "They did this to me! They did this to me!" She took off again, not caring how the concrete tore her sheer stockings.

Mike ran after her, picking up her shoes on the way, catching up easily, out distancing by a few strides and stopping her in her tracks, lifting her off the ground.

"Tell me. Tell me what they did."

"You don't need to know. You don't want to know." She had shut down as she always did when he got too close to what she was about. "Nobody knows. I don't want you, or anybody, to know."

"I want to know."

"I don't want you to know."

this can't be love

That was meant to stop him but it didn't work.

fourteen

"I've just told you how I feel about you. I've just let you know I like you the way you are. Why can't I know this thing about you that makes you special to me?"

"Will it change how you feel about me?"

"It might. I can't promise anything." He sat on a bench and held her on his lap, stopped talking and waited for her to speak.

The pipes played their dreary drone. Her head rested on his shoulder. She hardly breathed, humming the tune to the song they had danced to, whispering some of the words.

"I wasn't what they wanted." After a while, she said, "They wanted to fix me."

He remained still and silent, awaiting the next revelation.

"I can't feel what you feel. That was zapped out of me when I was fourteen."

"When you became a celebrity."

"I was the first girl in my school to have shock treatments."

"Electric shock?"

"Because they didn't want me to like boys."

Mike gave in to his impulse to touch her hair, stroking her head like he petted a puppy. When she didn't object, he rubbed his cheek against her temple. Getting no negative reaction to that, he cupped her face and tilted her chin to kiss her, enjoying her compliant response, hoping that, although she seemed passive, there was something going on deep inside that she did feel.

She wasn't indifferent to him. She was controlling, maybe involuntarily, everything she felt. Out of habit. Out of fear. A conditioned response. Her reaction to him in his office was proof enough that he could move her. The circumstances had to be right.

Soft lips, the slightest hint of longing eased between them. Mike held her, kissed her until he couldn't breathe. She stayed with him. Making allowances. Indulging him. Tolerant. He wasn't sure what it was but he took no liberties, made no sudden moves and ended the kiss with the same leisurely ease he'd started it.

Keeping her wrapped in his arms was about as hot as he could handle without going into his own freak-out. She was so beautiful he couldn't believe she was sitting in his lap, curling up like a child, snuggling in, as natural as though they'd been together for months. Mike pulled her closer, brought her knees in under his arm, settled his back against the bench, ready to stay right there all night if she wanted.

"As soon as everyone at school knew I was getting treatment, I was a freak."

"Teenagers are the worst for going after weakness," he said, pressing kisses on her temple and ear. She felt good. She smelled good. She had to know he wanted her. No way he could pretend he wasn't thinking about making love.

"Some of them were just curious. Some were scared I'd kill them. Some wanted to be just like me. And some hated me for being more 'popular' than they were."

"That seems about right for teenage behavior."

"I got smart pretty quick. At first, I fought back and made things worse. When I finally gave in, everyone left me alone. Except the boys."

This was it. The thing he had to hear, know and understand. He stayed quiet, stilled his hands, slowed his heartbeat, hugged her a little for reassurance, so she knew he was listening, he wanted to hear.

"The whole thing started because I had a picture in my wallet. My parents threatened the boy with jail if he came near me again. Then, they turned me over to the doctors." She was silent again.

Mike had nothing to say, no wisdom to offer, no questions of any relevance. Holding her and straightening the skirt of her pretty dress, kissing the top of her ear were enough.

"I learned a lot, especially how not to show I was scared."

His guts lurched. Everything he imagined that might have happened to her probably had. He hugged her tighter, pressed her head to his shoulder and waited. She shifted her body in the way that she danced on the stage, lithe and as effortless as water flowing down stream.

"The moment I had my high school diploma, I left. I saw my parents for the last time when I was twenty-one. They had disowned me by then, anyway, but I had a good lawyer."

"Aren't 'good' and 'lawyer' mutually exclusive?"

"Bad experience, Mr. Argent?"

"Divorce, Miss Hunter."

"I sued my parents for what they did to me. Since then, I've been on my own, the way I am." Before he could respond, she had pushed away and was standing in front of him. "This has been very nice but you need to get some sleep."

Mike tilted his head to look up at her, spread his arms along the back of the bench. "I'd rather stay here with you."

"You can't sleep in the park."

"I'm not going to sleep much anyway so it doesn't matter if I'm here or home."

She stepped nearer, standing between his knees, swaying on her bare feet. Mike steadied her with his hands on her hips. She didn't object.

"Are you going to sleep with me?"

Jakki stared beyond him toward the castle on the hill above them. She trembled and his hands shook.

"I know you've warned me but I don't see I'm completely off base, thinking you like me. Maybe not as much as I like you—."

"Why do you like me, Mike?"

"I feel good when you're around. Pure self-interest. I like the way you look. I like the way you dress. The way I see it, what's happened to you and to me has made us the kind of people who'll be good for one another."

"I can't be good for you, Mike. Not the way you need."

"Do you mind if I reserve judgment on that?" He stood, settled his back in the new position and wrapped his arms around her. The air had started to bristle. Before long, he'd be forced to admit he felt the pain that was always under the surface, obscured now by a real, more pleasant ache.

He closed his eyes, thinking through all the reasons he had for wanting to stay just like this, not have to move, not have to go back alone to his one bedroom flat, not have to take her back to the house in Musselburgh.

Not have to spend another night standing at the window, holding his back straight while spasms surged through him, making his nauseous. Not to dwell on why he'd spent the last six years getting as far away as he could from caring about anyone. Damned woman with crazy shoes got into him like no one else had ever done and he didn't want to get rid of her.

She wasn't wearing much to keep her warm. The velvet cape was enough before the sky went black and any residual warmth from the day had been driven down river. Hard as he tried, he wasn't much of a source of heat.

"I'd better get you home."

Something in the reflex, in her inhale, told him that going home wasn't what she wanted just then. His body told him, without dispute, taking her home wasn't what he wanted at all. Two rights don't always make a right but he was willing to risk being at least not wrong for another hour or more of being not alone. His body also told him that he needed to be moving or he'd be crippled all weekend.

"Matinee performance tomorrow?"

"Yes."

Without letting her go, he took a couple breaths. His first step wobbled but soon he had his stride and his pain under control, gesturing that he would carry her.

"I can walk."

"Your shoes are in my pockets." He stood still why she dug into his suit coat, bearing up none too well while she wriggled her hand in his pockets, oblivious to his lusty condition. Steadying her until she'd slipped into her shoes and her legs held her up without a wobble, with mixed feelings about losing her, slight burden as she was.

Jakki clasped his hand, laid her other hand on his arm for more support. He walked slower. No rush while he considered what else he could show her, besides his apartment.

Driving along the road to Musselburgh, he hoped for inspiration, glancing at his passenger as often as traffic allowed. It was a night for long drives and innocent revelry as the first week of the Fringe came to an end. This was his second Festival and the beginning of his second year working in Edinburgh on the Princes Street project. In a few months, the job was coming to an end. His company had already made suggestions for his next assignment. Until this past week, Mike hadn't thought or had any preference.

Her face was turned away from him, watching the tourists on the sidewalks, not registering any reaction to their antics, neither to approve nor mock. Acceptance? Tolerance? Or vacancy. No. She was far from vacant, he'd been wrong about that. She assessed and assimilated, but passed no judgment.

"Performance tomorrow night too?"

"Probably. Rache isn't much interested in the Saturday two-up so I'll do both."

He'd never felt he needed to ask permission to attend a performance. He didn't ask on this occasion either. He intended to be there. He guessed she knew that. Like she knew he wanted to be with her as often and for as long as he could. She had never invited him. That didn't mean he wasn't welcome.

He drove through the streets, catching glimpses of her at stop lights. Thought about all the ways she made him feel good. Happy, excited and thinking about a future, not just how to get through the next day. Like the song said. *No sobs, no sorrow, no sighs*. And the only dizzy spells were good. Trouble was, she wasn't thinking about a future, not with him.

He pulled the car up to the kerb a few doors down outside her house. Some of her house mates lounged in the front yard. When Jakki got out of the car, they turned to watch her. As she reached the gate, they formed a frontline defense.

The one Mike called 'Yeah' folded his arms. Mike clenched his jaw and squeezed Jakki's hand as Yeah said, "Gav's here. Your stuff is in the passage."

She raised her eyes to look beyond the three men. The roadster jerk, a big satisfied smirk on his face, stood in the passage beside a poorly packed trunk and half a dozen boxes with clothes and shoes spilling over the sides. A true citizen of the French Revolution, hiding behind his mob of bloodthirsty rabble.

Jakki dropped her hand from Mike's arm and walked forward but the three men didn't move. Gavin picked up a box and threw it over their heads followed by another with its contents flying in all directions.

"Don't! Please don't." Marie Antoinette to Gavin's Robespierre. Mike's girl had about as much chance against the jerk as the gracious, gentle and once-adored queen had against the savages who called themselves Citizens of the Republic. The mob waited for a sign from their First Citizen to riot.

Mike pushed through the wall of men and shoved the third box back into Gavin's face.

"I don't care who you are, mate, you're not treating anyone this way again. Put the damn box down and get out of my face before I break yours in every way possible."

"I'll have you arrested for trespassing."

"Go ahead. By the time the cops show up, you'll be hamburger." Mike caught Yeah by the neck. "If you know what's good for you, you'll get those cowards to help you carry

Jakki's belongings out to my car and wait there like good little boys."

"You can't—."

"Wanna bet? All I have to do is speed dial my crew and they'll use your skinny butt to sweep the street. Get moving." Mike let him loose. "And while you're at it, apologize to Jakki for being such assholes."

He turned back to Gavin and gestured for Jakki to come in. "Go up to your room and see if there's anything they left that you need. Gavin and I are going to have a wee conference."

While she was gone, Mike pressed his hand on the roadster jerk's chest and held him to the wall. "You have no idea how much I'd like to put you through this wall and the next, all the way to the next street and leave you for dead. I won't do it, not this time, because I'm a decent guy. You're not and it shows. One day, someone is going to teach you what you should have learned when you were a tike but it's never too late. Come near Jakki again and it may be my pleasure to set you straight."

"You think you're tough—."

"I know I am."

"My solicitor will be in touch, big guy."

"Good. Always nice to meet new and interesting people." He shoved his hand into his breast pocket. "And while I'm waiting, take this." He flicked Mary McEwan's business card in Gavin Andrews' face, slapping it against the roadster driver's collarbone.

Gavin flinched, rubbing his shoulder. He sneered back and jerked his head at his henchmen but no one prevented the construction site manager from tapping their leader on the cheek.

"Not so tough, are you, all on your own?"

Mike followed Jakki out, picking up a few stray garments as he did.

The three actors stood by the car, in a tight group, he guessed for safety. He unlocked the trunk and directed the packing. Jakki kept her back turned to her fellow cast members. They mumbled apologies as they passed and said something about the matinee.

Mike helped her into the car and drove away, nice and quiet, came to a stop near the river. "I have room at my place but if you have somewhere else you want to stay, I'll take you there."

She shook her head. He headed in the direction he'd wanted to go all evening.

At his building, he orchestrated the move of her trunk and boxes into his apartment. Once the boxes were stacked in the front room, he showed her the bathroom and the bedroom. Jakki followed him from room to room in silence, keeping close but not touching him. He gave her the bedroom, resigned to sleeping on the sofa. *Nothing new in that.*

"Where will you sleep?"

Clear enough to him that she was not going to give ground on that issue, not that night. To be honest, he hadn't thought beyond taking a few pills and stretching out the kinks. A few more nights on the sofa made little difference in his routine.

"Don't worry about me. Good night, darlin'." He shut the door and went into the kitchen. She took over the bathroom for a shower. By the time she was back in the bedroom, he had settled in front of the television, two pills and a glass of milk to wash them down already at work on his pain. He flipped through a few free-to-view channels, scrolled through the guide, watched the local news and a roundup of the Fringe for the week.

No surprise to him that *Bondage* got no mention—what had once been a grassroots, local showcase had long since become a side act to another celebrity circus, people he never heard of, didn't want to know. He muted the sound and allowed the images to mesmerize him but sleep didn't get him that night. As much as he stayed away from thinking about the girl sleeping in his bed, his mind dragged him back.

Not a lot of good was going to happen from thinking about her long legs, or soft bear cub fur on her head, or the funny way she dressed and looked so good to him.

Walking down the street with her on his arm made him proud. Watching her performance made him proud and humbled. Thinking about what she was doing with a guy like him made him feel lost. She had warned him enough. She wasn't going to stick. He thought about a future without her with him.

And if she wasn't with him who'd look after her? And if he wasn't with her, what was he going to do with the rest of his life? Bad enough he spent his days in dust and grime, he didn't want all his nights to be pills, television and the sofa.

fifteen

Not until the aromas of coffee and bacon worked their way to his brain was he aware that he'd fallen asleep and the sun had risen. *Sofa. Right. Nothing new.* One of his neighbors was up early for a change. Mike peeled one eyelid off his eyeball and looked through the window at the view of Edinburgh's hills, the long river to the bridge. Never failed to make him think of Florence or San Francisco. His frown pulled his brow over his eyes. He rolled his head on the back of the sofa.

One of his tank shirts danced around his kitchen to the music of Tommy Dorsey. *Right.* He would never let that shirt out of his sight again. Looked a hell of a lot better on that girl than on him. Bare legs and who knew what else. She had a piece of toast in her hand, taking bites as she did the two-step. He kept watching in silence so she would keep dancing while she cooked.

She swung and swayed, raised her arms, sang a few words, hummed and twirled, stopped dead in mid twirl and stared at her audience.

"You don't give a man much chance, do you?"

"How long have you been awake, Mike?"

"I can detect fresh coffee at nine hundred paces."

She smiled and returned to the work of the moment. "How do you like your eggs? And how many?"

"Sunny side up, two."

He tucked his shirt in where it had come loose, refrained from combing his fingers through his hair. "Have I got time for a shower?"

"Sure." She handed him a cup of coffee, poured milk in for him and stirred it, still swaying with the music. "Do you eat standing up or on the sofa?"

"The table is on the wall," he said, nodded in the direction. "Chairs are in that cupboard. I'll be about five minutes."

He returned, ready for work, with an empty cup. Jakki set a big plate with his eggs on the wall-table and sat opposite him with her own plate of eggs and grilled tomatoes. She wore a pair of his boot socks, sagging around her ankles. His tank shirt covered her from shoulders to knees, more than some of the outfits she wore. It was the fact she was wearing his clothes that caught him off guard, made him as speechless as a fourteen year old in front of his Religious Studies teacher. He laughed at the thought.

She cocked her head at him, pouting. "Are the eggs okay?"

"Great, no problem." He finished and pushed the plate away. "When do you need to be at the theater?"

"Same as usual."

"Need help getting there?"

She shook her head, took both plates to the sink and poured more coffee for him.

"I don't like leaving you on your own to get there with Gavin making a nuisance of himself."

"I can handle him." She took a few steps toward him. "Thank you."

"My pleasure. Close the door when you leave. It locks itself. I'll pick you up at the end of the show and give you a key so you can get in when you want. There's plenty of food—maybe nothing you like. I'll shop if you leave me a list. Use what you want. The place is yours." He spoke so fast he couldn't remember what he said, crinkled his brow to think. "I'm giving the rental back so I'll have the bike tonight." He looked straight at her, taking in her bare arms and legs, the shape of her breasts and hips, swallowed hard and grabbed his high visibility vest as he went out. His hair was still damp and the trickle of rain met no resistance, sinking in to soak him through.

Damn. She was one hell of a woman. She was wearing his clothes and sleeping in his bed, living in his place and cooking his breakfast. What more could he want? What more *did* he want? *Plenty.* He wanted plenty more. And, at the same time, he wasn't worrying about it. *Let it be. Let it happen. Natural.*

Jimmy grinned at him before Mike got the rental through the gate. The rental company clerk followed on his heels, inspected the car against his tick-sheet and drove away.

Saturday working had become the norm during the summer. Most of his crew needed the overtime and the job was behind schedule. Even calculating the Scottish weather into the project timeline, between the rain, the Fringe and the snow, they'd fallen a month behind.

They had daylight hours in the summer but these Fringe weeks brought their own delays with traffic snarls, wandering tourists and wayward performers. *Not forgetting the girls falling at your feet.*

A juggler tossed his three clubs in the air and danced around. The clock hadn't struck eight AM and already there were the blessed pipers, street artists and clowns wooing the intrepid out of their small change.

His thoughts took an easy left to think about his house guest at the same time as the joker from head office wiped his shoes on the Portacabin steps and pushed the door open.

Mike looked up the same time as Jimmy. Their eyes met and turned on Pete Ferguson. He didn't seem to notice while he searched through his briefcase. Mike sat back, drank from his coffee mug, nodded when Jimmy gestured about offering Ferguson a coffee.

"No thanks. I won't be long." He searched some more. "Sorry to bring this up, Argent, but we had a letter from the driver's solicitor."

"Today?"

"No. It was delivered by courier last night. I couldn't reach you."

"What'd he say?"

"Bullshit mostly. But we don't want any mishaps."

"What do you mean? Mishaps of what sort?"

"The driver claims that Miss Hunter or Jackson or whatever she calls herself is in some sort of con game to get money out of him. She's using you to get it."

Mike tossed his foreman a casual glance. Jimmy wasn't the only one of his crew who knew he'd taken Jakki Hunter on a date. Jimmy wasn't the vocal kind but Mike wasn't about to protest her innocence. Doing that would just alert Ferguson and head office to a possible conflict of interest. He didn't need a diagram to guess what they'd think if they knew he'd offered her a place to stay.

"Jimmy and I, half my crew here, saw exactly what happened, Pete. Not a lot either the girl or the driver can say to change the facts."

"It happened just the way we told you," Jimmy said and slurped his sugar-loaded coffee.

"Yeah. Yeah. I know all that but this solicitor says the woman's been hanging around here. Head office wants a clear road on this, Mike. That driver did some serious damage. They think the two of them are in it together, personal injury and what not. If she comes around again, call me."

"Sure," Mike said, "we're too dumb to read a crook when she hits us on the head."

"You know what I'm saying, Argent."

"I hear you. No problem," Jimmy said, "But you'll no convince me the lass is anything but a straight arrow."

"With respect, Macleod, I've seen her myself. She's not your conventional type."

Mike couldn't help his quick grin. Ferguson looked him in the eye and shook his head. "I don't want to come down hard on this, Argent. Stay clear. The driver's pulling every trick, son of some local hero. You know what that means."

"I get it, Pete, no fear."

When Ferguson retreated, Jimmy gave his boss a shrug and followed him out. Mike slapped his hard-hat on his head and his high visibility vest on his shoulders. While they stood together at the edge of the open pit, Jimmy cocked on eyebrow.

"Ha' you contacted Mary McEwan yet, Mickey?"

"Can't say I have. What's her angle?"

"Ach, you bloody Americans," Jimmy jeered, "always thinkin' because you're right, things'll work out. What you need is a barracuda who'll knock some sense into that laddie's skull and kick him and his sporran clear across Killiecrankie Gorge."

"I doubt Jakki will go for me taking the crew out to the jerk's place."

"They'd be happy to do that but that's no' what I'm suggestin', Mickey. I'm tellin' you, you need Mary McEwan."

"Tougher than this gang?"

"Not a man alive as tough as Mary. She'll take the lad, make him wish he'd never seen the long-legged lass—."

"You noticed them too?" Twinge of jealousy.

"—And have his gonads with chips for her dinner."

"Is this Mary some kind of roller derby queen?"

"Better. She's a parson's lass."

Mike's brows scrunched toward his nose but that didn't help decipher the local dialect.

"Takes on private work when she has a good reason. And I'll tell yuh, she'll love whippin' this lad's solicitah up the Forth and across the Firth, have his bits for her supper with a single malt chaser."

"That good?"

"That's why you're a lucky man, Mickey lad. She's my sister." The grin broke across Jimmy's face so wide and deep his craggy, weather beaten lines disappeared. "Damn lass married my best friend. Canna go a day without seeing her."

"So you think she'll help Jakki get rid of this jerk?"

"My wee Mary's been hankerin' for a chance to take on the lad's solicitah, ever since I told her about it. She's aching to bring 'em both down for all the world to see."

"What did they do to her?"

"Nothin' at all but be stupid. Any objections on the subject?"

"None I can think of. Your sister's probably going to receive a letter from the jerk's lawyer any time now. I slapped her card on him last night. Hope she doesn't mind we haven't met."

"Mary'll no mind. She'll be a-crowin'." Jimmy slapped his thighs, hooting out his approval. After he'd recovered, he asked, "Are you staying clear, Mickey?"

"Hard to do, Jimmy, but the less you know the better for you." Mike's expression twitched into a lop-sided smile and he walked back to his office, wondering what he was going to do when someone from head office found out he wasn't just seeing the girl. He wondered what he was going to do when he went to pick her up that night. The only thing he knew wasn't going to happen was staying clear. It was way too late for that.

Way too late.

The choke chain was embedded and he'd need surgery to dig it out. He didn't even want to do anything about it. He wanted to pick her up, take her home and let her take over his life. He sure wasn't doing anything interesting with it that couldn't be improved by Miss Hunter.

He got on with the work, half hoping she'd drop by before the matinee to bring him lunch or invite him to join her in the park. Instead, he wandered over to the nearest burger joint, got a man-sized meal with coffee and ate in his office, watching the street and letting his gaze meander toward the hill where she was onstage performing that dance while that fool, Yeah, mumbled his lines.

"Good time," Jimmy chuckled as he left the site. "I gave Mary the all clear. She's so fired up, she's offerin' to pay you for the privilege."

♥ ♥ ♥ ♥ ♥

sixteen

There was no one in that troupe of actors, except maybe the director—Terrence—who gave a damn about Jakki Hunter. Mike thought they actively disliked her but couldn't fathom why that was so. If he liked her, there was no reason he could think of that anyone else had any reason to dislike her. He was a better judge of character than most people he knew, especially after Margery taught him so many valuable lessons.

At the end of the day, he rode his bike around the city for a while, almost got himself knocked off at an intersection but pulled off in time to miss being broadsided by the bus. He still had time to kill before the end of the evening performance.

He debated whether to go home to shower and return. He tasted the grit of the city on his lips, felt its rasp on his face. He parked the bike in the alley and ran up the stairs. In the dark, he stumbled over the boxes stacked against the wall, flipped the light switch, stripped out of his work clothes, showered, dressed and was on his way out when he saw the note taped to the door. "I'll send someone to pick up my boxes."

The kick in his gut went straight to his chest, stopped his heart. The thud when the pump kicked back into thumping made him sick.

He looked around the room for any other signs. *Already. After less than a day. What pissed her off?* He didn't have any serious bad habits, no ugly character flaws, no fetishes.

He yanked the door open and slammed it behind him, crammed the helmet on his head and hit the streets like a hell-rider. He was not letting this happen.

Outside the theater, he waited until the audience came out. He counted six people as he pushed his way in.

Yeah slumped in a chair. Terrence stood at the stage. Rache sat on a barstool, swinging her legs.

"Where's Jakki?"

"You do not give up, do you, mate?" Yeah sneered.

Terrence turned and raised an eyebrow.

"Where is she?"

"Gone home."

"Not true." Mike jumped on the stage and ran down the stairs, calling her name, demanding she come out.

"I left you a note."

"Note? I don't call that a note. That was a sentence. No explanation. Not even a signature. What happened?"

"I can't stay there. With you."

"Why not? What's wrong with my place?" Safer than asking what he really wanted to know. What he had asked himself since the first time Margery had hit him. *What was wrong with him?* What about him got him taking up with the crazy ones, time after time?

Standing in front of him was the most delectable woman he'd known in a long time and she wasn't letting him anywhere near her. Was *he* the crazy one to keep wanting women who weren't good for him? Once that thought was in his head, he turned away.

"I guess you were right all along. But not for the reasons you thought."

Jakki gasped, covered her face but she didn't stop him from leaving.

Mike gave up resisting the urge and glanced over his shoulder. She wore some kind of white top that covered her to her midriff in the front and flowed to the floor at the back, some orange lamé leggings and suede shoes in all colors but none that matched her outfit. She surely stood out in a crowd and he was probably one of a few who knew she dressed in this crazy way for a better reason than seeking attention.

He turned in his stride. "What the hell, Jakki? If you think I'm like anyone else, you've got it wrong. I'm not ready for the big bust-up you have planned. No drama queen antics are going to get rid of me. I'm in your game for the long haul. Now, are you ready to go home?"

"Yes."

Mike took her hand and led the way back through the corridors under the church hall to the stage. He leapt down and lifted her off the stage, lowering her feet to the floor. "Those are pretty sassy shoes, darlin'."

When she smiled at him, he gave her a peck on the lips and dropped his arm around her waist. "Do you have a jacket?"

"In one of the boxes."

"You'll be warm enough in the overalls."

She nodded and said good night to her colleagues. Terrence, the only one who replied, waved and gave her a crooked smile. Mike's girl grinned back, turned on her heel with a flick of her hip and preceded him out to the street. As she got dressed for the ride, she braced her hands on his shoulders. He zipped her in, staring into her eyes. When she was encased, he pulled her close. "You're the craziest woman I've ever known. I'd rather be with you than anyone else in the world."

If he thought she might or expected her to reciprocate, he didn't show it. She lifted the passenger's helmet from the pillion seat and pulled it over her head, snapped the strap under her chin. Mike did the same with his headgear and mounted. When she was settled behind him, he ignited the engine and gave it some throttle.

She wound her arms around his chest and leaned against his back, fitting herself to his spine like a second skin.

Mike took time to adjust his body to the sensation of intimate contact and rolled away from the kerb. At the bottom of the hill, he turned left and moved through the damp streets, his bike purring in harmony with the pipes and laughter.

Jakki laid her head on his shoulder blade and made no remark when he turned in the direction of the Musselburgh road, along the Firth and out into the countryside.

The dark road offered no relief to the ache in his heart, answered none of his doubts, nor gave him any sense of peace. By the time they had climbed the hill overlooking the city, Mike had settled his argument with himself and pulled off the road to a layby, cutting the engine when they were at the viewpoint.

He held his helmet in his lap and followed the lights of the traffic flowing along Princes Street. After a few minutes, Jakki also removed her helmet.

"Do you want to tell me what that was about?" Certain she knew what he meant and certain she would make up her mind in her own time whether to tell him, Mike observed the capital city in silence.

The traffic moved and halted at regular intervals as the lights changed at intersections. The second weekend of the Fringe was marked by a few noisy fireworks, a fun fair of rides to entertain the local teenagers and a procession of pipe and drum bands. Mike exhaled in relief he was far enough away to be spared the clatter and drone.

Probably the one in twenty-nine thousand people who found no listening pleasure in the bagpipes, being a crusty musical grump didn't rate high on his radar.

Gnawing at his insides, highest on his list of reasons he wasn't going to sleep too well? Being in love with Jakki Hunter for no damned good reason he could grasp.

But he was and he had to deal with it. He wasn't trying to figure out what made her tick. He'd pretty much come to terms with that.

She was messed up. She had quirks. Nothing he couldn't live with. She was smart. She was unique. She needed a warden. She didn't talk much. She wasn't immune to him. She showed no signs that she was ever going to want him.

Who was the crazy in the duo?

Mike laughed—a sharp snort of self-derision. *Crazy?* Pretty much all the time with her close to him and wanting her closer. He wanted her so much closer, she'd be inside him. To his way of thinking that was a done deal. He wanted to turn the tables but he figured he couldn't do that without something dramatic that would hurt her and he wanted none of that. *Crazy.*

"You know I want you, don't you?" It was a real question, asked to get an answer.

"Yes."

Progress? Not exceptional, not reciprocal, not a declaration. What had he expected? He'd known well before he made his confession she wasn't on the same page and more than likely wouldn't be any time soon, if ever. Mike claimed he was nothing like Gavin. He claimed he'd never throw her away. *Leave her?* He didn't want that either, not then and maybe not for a long while.

"Gavin's attorney contacted me."

Mike wasn't surprised. He turned his head, encouraging her to say more.

"Gavin must have told him I was seeing you. He asked a lot of questions and wanted to know my address for when the insurance company took my statement." She rested her chin on his shoulder blade, exhaled a long sigh. "I'm not as dumb as Gavin thinks. He's going to use my staying with you against your company."

"One of the guys at HQ told me the same thing."

"So you see why I can't stay at your place."

"No, I don't. You being at my place is after the fact, no bearing on the incident at all. Gavin's still a jerk with a car."

"You could lose your job."

"If I was worried about that, I'd ask Jimmy to shoot me." That was true. Truer than he wanted to admit. "I have a lawyer too. She's going to clean the streets with your friend, Gavin."

She turned her head so her cheek pressed against his shoulder blade.

"What do you want to do tonight? Any sights you want to see, darlin'? Places you want to eat?"

"I'd like to go home."

Mike didn't ask. He rolled the bike in a slow arc and headed back to the city. At the door of his building, Jakki waited with her arms wrapped around her chest while he stowed the bike in the garage. He slipped the key into her hand and stood behind her, tempted to put his arms around her. He followed up the stairs to his floor and into the apartment.

As soon as the door closed, she turned on him. "I'll pay half the rent and cook."

"I'll pay half the rent and clean."

She offered her hand and he sealed the contract with a shake.

"What's for dinner?"

Now that his back ached less, their arrangement of the previous night was less satisfactory. The door to his bedroom closed with a sigh and a definite click that reverberated in his ears even though he faced the window and had been contemplating the view over the river through all the time she showered.

The kitchen was spotless—his contribution to the contract honored the moment he finished the best meal he hadn't cooked on that old stove since he moved in and realized he had to do something energetic when the idea of thanking her in another way came to mind.

She gave him no opportunity to misinterpret—willfully—any of her actions. Miss Hunter was not in his apartment, living with him, sleeping in his bed, because she wanted a relationship, not a physical one at any rate.

He was all right as long as he understood on her terms, but his terms were in another stratosphere. Not for the first time, he wondered what she did want. He had an easier time knowing what she didn't want. Top of that list was him. Okay to lean on, catch a lift, twist around, use, even depend on. Like a big brother.

He wasn't thinking of her as his little sister when he took his turn in the shower. His imagination was way out in space the moment he caught the scent of her soap in his olfactory nerves. He picked up the bar and compared it to his shower gel. Soap won the sexy rating. He let it slide back onto the tray and filled his palm with lime tea tree or whatever the buy-one-get-one-free wash was, kept his thoughts far away from sharing a shower experience with his house guest but she crept in anyway.

Shows I'm still alive. Going out for a bit, trying his luck at the local pub, bringing another guest home wasn't going to happen. Staying out wasn't an option.

Resigned to a quiet night and a bit of sleep, Mike sought his usual refuge on the couch when his comfort demanded. He couldn't sleep lying down in any position when his back gave him trouble. Too much pain made sleep in any position impossible even with a good pain killer. He was a fan of digital free-view, hated cable and satellite. Grumpy old guy at thirty-one.

He slumped back on the sofa, grabbed the remote and began the channel-flipping ritual.

One good date, a few kisses and it was over but he kept telling himself he wasn't like those other guys but here he was thinking about ways to get out of the situation. *Hell.* He couldn't do that. *Hell.* He couldn't do this either.

seventeen

"Are you sleeping?" He had tapped on the bedroom door twice. He tapped again, louder. When she opened the door, he stepped back, struck dumb and gaped at her with her hair sticking up in every direction, barefaced, so fresh and clean she looked like a kid. A tom-boy with the most beautiful legs and lips he imagined kissing, tasting, feeling against his skin.

She didn't say anything. He couldn't say anything. Any second he was going to lose control. Any second he was going to make a fool of himself.

"I don't mind sleeping on the sofa if you want your room." She leaned her head against the edge of the door.

"Not the room." He braced his hands on the doorjamb. "You. I want you."

She pressed her lips together, not in doubt or anger. "I'm sorry."

"Not going to happen, right?"

"Maybe we'd better talk."

"Maybe so."

She came out of the bedroom in a thick terry robe, his socks drooping around her ankles. Mike followed her to the sofa but when she sat in the center, facing the big window overlooking the sparkling city, he stood at the arm, watching her. Jakki curled her legs under her and folded her arms around her chest, rubbing her hands along her ribcage.

"Cold?"

"A little."

He brought an afghan from the other chair and she curled into it, looking up at him. After a moment, she turned her attention to the window. In the dark, as they were, the lights from the city below twinkled like stars in the rain-lashed sky. Mike thrust his hands in his pockets.

"Thank you for telling me."

"It's nothing you haven't heard before, right? The kind of thing you'd expect." Junk yard dog whining.

"Pretty much," she agreed.

"Not dazzling with originality." His moping and hound-dogging were getting on his nerves. The choke chain was tighter every time he opened his mouth. "I've got to say this whether you want to hear it is not my problem. You are the weirdest, strangest, most exasperating, intriguing woman I've ever met and I cannot imagine, do not even want to contemplate, my life without you. So here it is. I love you."

She covered her face with her hands.

"Not what you wanted to hear? Too soon? You think I'm crazy. Probably. That's the only way I can explain what I feel. I love you and if you can't handle it or don't want to, I have to live with it but when I think about not having you around, even if it's just as friends, I can't handle that. I want to take care of you, be around to make sure you get home, help you walk in those stupid shoes, whatever you need. I'm not like those other guys. Maybe that makes me a fool but I'll take you on your terms, Jakki. Friends, whatever you want. I love you. I don't want to be without you."

She buried her face on her knees and covered her head with her arms.

"That bad?"

She shook her head, whimpered.

"That good?"

She nodded.

"What does that mean? We're good? You'll stay? What?"

She wiped away the tears on her face with her fingers. "I don't know what to do. This has never happened to me before. What am I supposed to do, Mike?"

He could tell her what he wanted her to do. He could pretend he didn't know she didn't know how to respond. He could forget her wiring had been fried a long time ago. Instead, he said, "You'll figure it out."

"What if I get it wrong?"

"There is no wrong, darlin'. That's the beauty of someone loving you." He reached out a hand. "Come on, I've kept you up past your bedtime."

"Do you want to sleep with me?"

Mike chuckled and kissed her fingertips. "As a euphemism that has always puzzled me. I don't want to sleep—couldn't right now anyway and what I do want to do is beyond my endurance level tonight."

"Why?"

He stretched his hand to the small of his back. "Giving me trouble right now."

Jakki threw off the afghan and was on her feet, darted behind him and planted hands on his shoulders. "Lay on the floor, face down."

"What are you doing?"

"I worked in a massage parlor," she said. "I'm pretty good at this."

"Somehow, I don't think that sort of massage is going to help."

"I'm serious. I took a course. I really am a masseuse. Take off your t-shirt."

"Now, wait a minute—."

"Don't be silly. I know what I'm doing."

When he hesitated, she pushed his hands out of her way and hiked up his t-shirt. He stopped her and took a long breath.

"I'm not going to hurt you. I need to work on your lower back."

Mike shook his head in disbelief, calming his agitation and finished removing his shirt. She trotted into the bedroom, he returned to the window, forcing himself to concentrate on his pain and keep his imagination away from being half-undressed and her being in his bedroom wearing his t-shirt and socks.

All his effort to be a decent friend came to an end when she trotted back, her arms full of towels and lotions and oils, dressed in leggings and a sports top, ready for a workout. She spread the towels over sofa cushions on the floor and directed him to lie on his belly while she set out all the bottles on the coffee table.

"Relax."

He grunted something like acquiescence but when she straddled his back and sat on his thighs, he shut his eyes so hard, his head ached.

"Don't try. Just do it. Relax or this won't help."

He fought the urge to turn over and take her by surprise. The battle took its toll on his pain threshold.

She poured oil into her hands and worked them over his back as if she was covering him with sunscreen. She took another, more pungent oil and spread that over his shoulders. When she dragged her fingers down the middle of his spine, he felt the strength in her hands right through his back to his belly and into his groin like a caress. He groaned, giving himself up to want and need and letting her have her way with him.

The combined scents of the oils were a drifting pleasance that won out over his tension enough to relax a few muscles, except for one, but as she worked on his back, Mike become less concerned about his heightened state. His thoughts lost direction, mesmerized by repetition. He was only semi-conscious, fatigue trampling his last reserves, when she leaned over and kissed his mouth. His eyelids were closed. As reality clawed him back from the oblivion of sleep, his lips parted in a brief smile.

"Why did you do that?"

"I felt like it," she sighed. "Is that okay?"

"Sure," he yawned, "as long as I get to feel like it once in a while." The kiss was sweet, a peck, but voluntary—not a stunned response to something he did. She felt like kissing him. Of all the things he had imagined, this was a block-busting, show-stopper of a moment.

"You feel like it all the time."

"Can you blame me?" He yawned again and there was no sign of his earlier preparedness.

"I don't want that."

His eyes stung, lids drooping with a need to shield his eyes from the lights from the streets. He wanted to ask if she knew what she wanted but his jaw muscles were slack and his brain swirled in a purply-orange.

"I want to be the one who feels like it for a change."

He grinned in his hazy, orangey-grape-colored and lavender-scented hazard zone, raised the fingers of his right hand in a gesture of acquiescence but nothing else moved.

eighteen

Benny Goodman's horn and the swing of lyrics so familiar he sang along before he heard the words. He felt for the remote, realizing he'd slept on the floor, on cushions, with nothing but the afghan over his hips. Turning onto his back, careful not to dislodge afghan covering his mid-quarters, surprised he wasn't stiff and more surprised when his turn was impeded by a lump smacked up against him. Mike took a moment to assess.

Not the base of the sofa. Not the stereo cabinet. Solid but not geometric. Soft bits but not inanimate. *A girl*. One quick glance over his shoulder that didn't hurt. His girl. *Okay. Still asleep.* Still a chance to make an excuse for whatever he did. *Apologize.*

Too late. She stretched. Her long body all along his spine, down his hips, cradling his thighs, her knees bending into his, bare feet and toes curling at his ankles. A long sigh, stirring the wisps of hair on his nape. And her arm sweeping over his shoulder and embracing his chest. Those strong fingers caressing his mid line.

Pure blissful torment. He didn't dare move.

She raised her torso to lean against him and peered down at him. He stared straight at the window sill, too late to pretend he was asleep. Too late to conceal the major damage she was doing to his good intentions.

"Good morning, Mike. How did you sleep?"

"Good. Thanks."

"You kind of passed out."

"Must have been tired."

She raised herself higher to lean over him, resting her chin on his upper arm, while her hand played over his chest. Mike wasn't certain he was breathing then but when her hand slid over his belly, he stopped altogether, swallowed hard, near bursting.

"I think you must have been exhausted," she said. "No matter what I did, you slept right through it." Her fingers reached his lower belly, played him like a guitar, strumming his skin.

"What did I miss?" Somehow, he turned onto his back and she slid up next to him, slotting her shoulder under his arm, pressing her breasts into his ribs. She had removed her sports top and leggings but was hidden from view though her softness and warmth, the slight moistness of their bodies surrounded him.

"I confess I took advantage of you, but nothing happened."

"I'm not much of a party animal when I'm unconscious."

She dropped her head onto his shoulder and he ventured to raise his hand to cradle her head, instinct guiding him to give her all the moves.

"You did all right."

Mike laughed. "Good to know I can behave when comatose. Reassuring somehow. If I'm ever in the hospital again."

"I didn't say you behaved."

"Unbecoming a gentleman?"

For answer, she wiggled her fingers along his hip.

"What are you planning, Jakki?"

"Let me know if I do anything you don't like."

He endured her scrutiny, curiosity, examination, experimentation and research until she had exhausted her imagination – without once raising any barriers or doubts. Her innocent intent made him laugh and he was certain she intended to drive him to the edge of insanity but he had promised not to interfere or to retaliate, or reciprocate.

As much as he wanted to explore her, this was her expedition. She didn't want a travelling companion. The most he could do was lift his hand to touch her hair, until her body trembled and she sobbed, curling into his side.

"Jakki," he whispered, turning to cradle her, pulling her bare legs against his thighs. "Jakki. Darlin'." He held her head against his shoulder. "Hush now. It's okay. Nothing to worry about." Mike kissed her forehead and cheek, absorbing the tremors wracking her body. They subsided until they were intermittent and slight, her sobs quieting to sniffles and silence. A painful silence.

She was small and soft and lying in his arms as he had imagined in his dreams, all he wanted and unavailable. Maybe he should be mad, feel cheated, frustrated – but he didn't. Just a vague sense of relief, a small triumph.

He lifted her chin and brushed his lips over her mouth, stroked her bear-cub hair, kissed her lips again taking the scent of tears into his lungs, tasting her wet cheek on his lips, returning to her mouth, pressing her closer to him, tracing his tongue over the edges of her teeth, into her mouth.

Her lips widened to accept his invasion, her whole body unfurling in a long sensual movement as subtle and supple as a sigh when he settled between her thighs, pressing tentatively against her, surprised she opened, warm and moist, accepting this invasion with no resistance.

He raised his body and stared down at her in wide-eyed realization.

"You didn't tell me. You should have told me. If I'd known—."

She covered his mouth with her hand, still wide-eyed, swallowing hard and taking deep breaths.

"Are you okay, sweetheart?"

A nod.

"Do you want me to stop?"

She shook her head and glanced away. A shrug. Too late for protection. Fool. He eased deeper, holding back the urge to thrust. Consequences. *Yeah. Right.* So perfect. She winced. He groaned. Wrong. He kissed her neck, thrust into her mouth again. No regret. No restraint.

She pushed back. Long bare legs wrapping around him, cradling his hips, holding him. All the encouragement he needed. Jakki had other plans. He straightened his arms and gazed down at her.

"What is it, darlin'?"

"Are you mad?"

"Why on earth do you think I'd be mad?"

"You said I should have told you. I'm sorry I didn't. It's just that I wasn't sure. Not before last night."

He got it, understood her silence and felt only a little less ashamed of himself than he would have if he had still thought what the other men in her life assumed—that she was easy for everyone except him.

"Why me? Why did you choose me?"

"My parents got one thing right but not because they were right to fix me for something I never did. I learned no one was going to take care of me but me. Unless they really loved me. You said you did. I believed you. I do believe you."

He bent his arms enough to kiss her forehead, reigniting his interest in what was going on in his works. He nudged her chin up so he could reach her mouth, sank deeper, deeper, wandering through, finding curves and hollows he hadn't kissed before, feeling every inch of her over every inch of him.

He didn't ask if she felt the same about him, figuring she did but wouldn't be able to define or evaluate those feelings in any way that was meaningful to her. She wanted to kiss him. She wanted him to make love with her. She seemed to enjoy giving her body to him.

If she told him then that she loved him, he'd know that she was saying what she thought he wanted to hear. True. He did, but her acquiescence in her "ruin" said a whole lot more.

This is what had driven other men crazy—their assumption she was holding back from them something she had given to others. That had started to drive him crazy, thinking about his girl with Gavin when she refused to be with him. And all the time, she was doing what she could to protect herself from guys who only wanted sex, guys not so different from him.

While he was lying on the floor with the sun poking him in the eye, he thought about Gavin, what he'd done just because she didn't put out. Hanging was too good for a guy like that. He had to ensure nothing like that happened to her again.

"Where do you have to be today, darlin'?" He pulled her close and tilted her chin. "Anything special?"

"Is it Sunday?"

"Maybe. I have to be at the site most of the day. Whatever day it is. Tight deadline now."

"If it's Sunday, I'm free until five. Just one performance."

"Do you feel okay?"

She turned into his arms, hiding her face in his shoulder. "Yes."

"Regrets?"

"What do you feel, Mike?"

He considered accusing her of avoiding his question but that would be avoiding hers. "I feel good. I feel sorry because I was unfair to you. I made assumptions—exactly what I accused other men of doing. Not the best man for you by a long way but proud you think so. At least good enough to trust to be your first lover. Funny thing about that, though."

"What's funny about it?"

"I want to be your only lover."

She didn't move or say anything for so long, he thought she'd fallen asleep. When he turned his head, he saw she was crying, silent tears, spilling out of her eyes, into the tufts of hair at her temples.

"Is that so terrible, Jakki?"

"I don't understand. Why do you want that?"

♥ ♥ ♥ ♥ ♥

nineteen

He worked through what he knew, wading in the minefield that was her emotional mix up.

"I guess that is a pretty scary outcome if you're not sure what you feel about someone. But I am sure, and wanting to be with you, only you, comes naturally in that scenario. Maybe some men play on the whole polygamy myth, makes them feel good about their immaturity but for most of us, one good woman is plenty—more than I deserve. I want you to be my one and only. When you're ready, you may want the same. Until you do, I can promise I won't stray. I'll appreciate knowing if you have plans for us."

"I'm not…I mean I feel like this is where I want to be. But I don't know, Mike. What if something happens? What if you have to go? What if I have to go?"

"Let's do this a day at a time," he said, holding her trembling body. "Today, we're together. The two of us. I'm committed to that."

"Me too," she said, trembling subsiding, sigh of relief, releasing to calm. "Me too."

Riding into the site at seven AM, clean shaven, a full night's sleep to sustain him and an hour of making love to a woman he was hankering to see again gave Mike Argent an air of contentment he hadn't felt since his first day on a new job— his first job.

Contentment didn't account for his down deep crowing. He had the woman he wanted. The junk yard dog was top dog, leader of the pack.

How long this was likely to last was anyone's guess and not his decision. Jakki Hunter was as likely to walk out in ten minutes as she was likely to stay for ten years. If there was anything strange in his choice to stay, it was not finding anything strange about it at all.

Plenty of people committed to another person with no guarantee they would see their loved one again. Too many things got in the way. What made the difference was the effort. This girl could mess him up bad but she wouldn't intend to. Making sure she was all right with him was his job, one day at a time. If she wasn't there when he got home, he'd know where to look. If she didn't come back to him after the performance, he'd find out why and figure out what to do then.

The difference was that she gave him enough. He could live with quirks and uncertainty and crazy shoes. He looked forward to whatever came next.

When he left his apartment, she still slept. He thought about that through the first hours of the day and then he thought about how long her legs were and how he felt making love. Nothing prepared him for the day long separation. At the end, he did what he had done since he bandaged her arm. Mike went home, got cleaned up and rode his bike to the theater.

He found a place to park his bike, blueberry and raspberry swirls all accounted for. He walked through the crowds of theater goers, street performers and pipers, watched a few performances on corners and bought a ticket to *Bondage* — a regular patron. He took a seat in a different part of the theater and ordered a beer before the performance began. Another group of patrons arrived after him, making a decent audience of several more than the first night he had watched.

The new audience was intent on their orders of alcohol when the performance began. Jakki Hunter took her position at the apron, dancing in silence as she had most other nights during the play's run. There was no difference, no before or after recollections to discern.

Her movements mesmerized him and quieted the drinkers, as she did every night. The difference was in him. Mike watched the audience, particularly the men and didn't wonder at their captivation. Her body made promises, offered possibilities but her ambience was forbidding—an aura of untouchable perfection, too good, too perfect, too unattainable.

The women ignored her—for the same reasons.

He had no urge to leap to his feet and lay claim, gloat, crow, flaunt his prize. No, he was content to have a private understanding of her and of his place in her life. He had no need or wish to go public.

He didn't pretend to own or possess. He was happy to watch her and not let her secret be known. He was her secret. That thought made him laugh. A great hulk like him the secret lover of a nymph.

As the performance came to the end, the audience stirred, ordering drinks, raising their voices, commenting amongst themselves. Mike pushed his glass around the table, blocking the noise, refusing the temptation to eavesdrop. He hadn't committed himself to any attempt to understand the play. Any comments he did hear were as incomprehensible out of context as any snatched conversation.

"You are some kind of masochist. Either that or plain stupid. Can't figure it at all."

Mike lifted his gaze from the rim of the glass to study Gavin's sneer but made no adjustment to his own expression.

"Here you are, night after night, hanging on every line and you still don't get the message."

"Seems to me you have the same problem. Or is it that you're here because I am? Some kind of crush on me?"

"I *own* this show. You get that? I'm an investor. I'm making money every night. Every time she rings some bloke's chimes, I get richer. Get it. She works for me."

That he didn't know. Should have guessed. Mike leaned back in the chair, hooked his thumbs in his pockets, kept his eyes on Gavin's face. The guy had a funny way of handling his investments. Mike shrugged, pushed away from the table and stood up, tossing a few bills on the beermat for the waitress.

Gavin shoved the table into Mike's legs and grinned when the glass smashed on the floor.

"There go your profits for tonight," Mike said, sweeping the bills into the waitress's hand, keeping her from picking up the broken glass. "I don't know what your problem is, but seems you're a sore loser. Whatever you think you own, it makes no sense breaking it in some kind of tantrum. Show's over. Curtain's down."

"She won't stay with you."

"I don't know why you're so concerned about me. Nice to know you care, all the same." Mike walked to the side of the stage and helped Jakki down, winked at Gavin and shadowed her out of the building. She didn't offer any explanation for Gavin's presence and Mike didn't ask. By the time they were in front of his apartment, with her arms wrapped low around his waist, he'd forgotten all about the confrontation.

He handed her the spare key and followed her up the stairs to the entrance. Jakki stared at the key in her hand, looked at him. After a while, a soft smile curved her mouth and she opened the door. Mike stood at the open door as she put the key on the hall table, unbuttoning her bolero jacket with Hawaiian flowers all over it. What had giving her the key have to do with making her happy? She danced into the kitchen and danced out again.

"Something to eat, Mike?"

"If you're fixing, I'm eating, darlin'."

"I'm fixing." She be-bopped around the small room, pans, ladles, wooden spoons, steaks and green beans flying around in exuberance. Mike pulled his bike jacket off his shoulders and tossed it on the sofa, joined her between the counter and the fridge, took out a beer and twisted the cap off.

"Does that jerk own your show?"

"If you call losing money ownership."

"Investor?"

"Benefactor."

That explained everything. The jerk backed the show and wanted some return on investment. Wasn't getting it.

"Are you getting paid?"

"None of us are. Everyone has to pay their way. Otherwise we couldn't be here." She tossed lettuce and green olives in a bowl, sliced some red onion.

"What do you get out of it?" He chugged down the brew, set the bottle on the drainer, out of his league in the scheme of her life.

"Experience. This is a great testing ground for new work."

Mike folded his arms across his bulky chest, thought about reaching for her and kept his hands to himself.

"We haven't been getting the audiences we hoped for but those who've come have given us good reviews."

"What do they say?" *Mistake. Wrong question.* He waited for the result.

"What do you think of the play, Mike?"

Perfect. Opened the door on that blast furnace all by himself. "Honest answer?"

She nodded, ducked her head into the fridge and brought out salad dressing, dribbled it around the lettuce.

"I don't get it." Even a junk yard dog could have done better, come up with something. "I've watched the play four, five times and I'm still mystified." *Honest? Not even close.* "It's a jumble of words to me." *Closer.* "To be perfectly truthful, I keep my eyes on you. Everything else is over my head." He'd done it with that. She didn't say a word, tossed the salad and set the bowl on the counter. "You're the best thing about it. The only thing that makes any sense."

"Do you want another beer?"

Tone. Sarcasm. He waited for her to snap his head off. "I come to see you, make sure you're okay. Take you home safe." *Push it.* He was on that downward rollercoaster drop. No stopping the fall. "Otherwise I'm mystified. Like you want me to feel dumb."

"Do you think other people see it that way?" She squirted Ranch dressing in swirls around the contents of the salad bowl.

"Is that what you wanted, darlin'?"

"It's how I feel. Every day. I wake up 'mystified' and feeling 'dumb'. If that's how *Bondage* makes you feel, I didn't intend for anyone to be hurt. Is that bad, Mike? Did I do it wrong?"

"Were you honest, Jakki? Was this you?"

"I think so. I wrote what I felt. I wrote the story the way it came out. I don't know what I wanted. I was tired of being alone."

Mike covered his eyes, took a deep breath. Extending his arm, he drew her close, rested his chin on the top of her head. "It's not wrong, darlin', it's brave. It's what you have to do. I don't know a damned thing about what you do. I've never written anything but a tick sheet report. But, I know something about how you feel. That's good. You did your job."

"Gavin said I should explain everything so the audience knew how messed up I was."

"Glad you didn't listen to that piece of—."

"Don't." She clapped her fingers over his lips. "Do you want to eat here or on the sofa?"

"What do you think of the play?"

"What do you want, Mike? I asked you what *you* thought."

"Now, I'm asking you."

"I have enjoyed working with Kevin, Terrence and Rache. All the cast. I've learned a lot about performance and the mechanics of drama. The play is experimental. I'm an amateur and could use the help of a more experienced dramatist. But for a first effort, not that bad."

"Don't be so hard on yourself. Like you told Rache." Mike lowered his chin, peering at her with his head cocked, gave her a slight nod. "How would you change it, darlin'?"

"I'd make it more honest, not hide behind that 'difficult poet syndrome'."

"I've watched the play, and you, all this week. I've been with you most days and nights." He straightened his spine and held her a little away. "I've learned enough about you to recognize you in every word. It's a brave thing to tell your story, darlin', and let people see into your soul but any more honest won't be for your own good." Mike ducked his head to look up into her eyes. "You know where you are. The audience doesn't have to know any more than what they understand."

"That's not honest."

"There's honest, darlin' and there's self-destruction."

Mike kissed the peak of her forehead, kept his arms loose in the embrace, nuzzled her temple. Any other words of wisdom he uttered would be wrong.

"I trust you, more than I ever trusted anyone, even my brothers."

He acknowledged her statement with a nod, exhaled a long breath.

"You're the only one I've ever let this close."

twenty

He tightened his arms and let go. The way he saw it, she didn't let him that close, not as close as he needed, not at close as she thought. *Eggshells.* Full, blown up close was in the future. *Maybe.* Not forever but not tomorrow either.

When she had been silent for several moments, he kissed her mouth.

"Salad's getting cold, darlin'."

He filled their plates and took another beer, waited for her to decide where she wanted to be. He followed her to the sofa.

"How many brothers?" She'd never spoken of them before. He'd thought all along she was an only child.

"I don't want to talk about them."

Mike swallowed a mouthful of salad, poured beer down his throat. "My folks never had any other kids. No special reason for that I ever found out about."

"You're lucky."

"You learn to like your own company and how to make friends fast."

"My brothers hate me. I haven't seen or spoken to either one since I won the lawsuit—no, since I filed the lawsuit."

"You can't choose your family."

"You can leave them."

"You can." He finished the salad and lay back, swirling the beer in the bottle while she considered.

"I did. I'm glad I did."

Mike switched the bottle to his other hand before he clasped her fingers and raised them to his lips. "You have every reason to be proud."

"I'm not proud. I'm sorry. And scared."

What could he say? Making vows and promises wasn't in his best interests at that moment, would not mean what he wanted her to understand. He moved closer and put his arm around her, his hand on her hip.

"What's it to be, Jakki? Some mindless show or bedtime?"

"When you put it that way," she said, her free hand wandering close to his equipment, "I'll take mindless show."

He reached for the remote but she took it away from him and leapt from the sofa. He grinned at her playful waggling of the remote and be-bopping in front of him, stretched out his hand and caught her around the knees. She fell on top of him exactly as he intended, her arms and legs every which way. Mike flipped her onto her back and planted his hips between her thighs, staring down at her big eyes. "Mindless enough?"

She answered with her hands, working their way through the labyrinth of cloth, hide and studs to free him. When her fingers settled, his whole body hissed like water in hot oil. With one hand, he pulled away her silk panties and, while he slid into her, he pulled off the rest of her clothes, tossing them aside. She hummed as he stroked her, throwing her arms over her head, defenseless and complicit in her surrender.

Tentative, uncertain but present, she scraped her fingers over his chest. Her breath caught, eyes wide, body rigid until it vibrated, silencing the hum for a long moment—the moment he gave in to her demands, burying his face in her neck. She laughed.

"Thank you," he murmured.

His partner in bliss sighed, "Too mindless?"

Monday morning, Mike woke at five, to be at the site by six. Tempted to wake her to say good bye and wish her a good day, he reconsidered. She slept so peacefully, he left a note on the table and rode through the dripping streets to work.

Mid-morning, he phoned the apartment but got no answer.

Jimmy walked across the yard, hands stuffed in his pockets, his high-viz vest pushed back, his hard hat cocked and the strap dangling, flopping around his chin. One of the other men walked beside him, both talked and gestured until they stood outside the Portacabin office. Mike finished his paper work and joined them, a mug of coffee in his hand.

Before any of them said another word, a car careened into the yard, spewing gravel and mud from its skidding wheels.

"What is it about these city boys?" Mike set his mug on the step and stalked toward the car, studying the driver and the passenger. "Unbelievable." He opened the door and reached in. Jakki took his hand and pulled herself out. The driver spun out and was gone before she was fully balanced, but Mike had a good grip on her.

Eyes wide and hands shaking, she stared at him. Mike wrapped his arm around her waist and walked her toward the site office.

Jimmy greeted her as if her arrival by screeching car was as ordinary as a crew member walking through the gate carrying a lunch box and his tools. Jakki smiled but didn't venture to speak.

Mike handed her a cup of tea with milk, holding back his questions, waiting for an explanation. She held the cup tight in both hands, the trembling coming to a slow end. When no sign she was going to fill him in on her latest escapade was forthcoming, Mike left her in his office and returned to the site, stood beside his foreman but was no more forthcoming than his girlfriend. Jimmy gave him a sly look but ventured no further than a tsk and a shake of his head before going back to the work.

In less than five minutes, the phone in his office rang and the hand held receiver beeped in his pocket.

"What do you think you're doing?"

"My job mostly. Why do you ask, Pete?"

"That jerk's solicitor is all over us here. Threatening to sue us into oblivion. Tell me one thing, Argent, is that nutcase still hanging around?"

"By 'nutcase,' do you mean the innocent victim of that jerk's vicious assault?"

"That's what I'm talking about, Mike. This company cannot be seen to be taking sides in this. He's already shouting about conspiracies and fraud. He's claiming you and that crazy woman cooked up this scheme to swindle his client."

"Just who is the crazy one? I never met the woman 'til that jerk pushed her out of his car."

"Tell me in all honesty, Mike, are you seeing her?"

"Yeah, I see her." Mike met Jimmy's stare.

"How often?"

"Most days. She works up the road, can't miss her."

"What about nights?"

"Most nights."

"What's going on with you? Didn't you get the message?"

"I got it, but I don't see what the big deal is. And don't bother explaining. What's going on here is no one's business but mine. If you need an independent witness, Jimmy was right there, beside me, saw everything I saw."

"I'm advising you to stop whatever is going on with you and this woman—."

"And I'm telling you, no. That's not going to happen."

"I hope you don't regret your decision, Mike."

"Thanks. I won't." He disconnected and stared off across the site.

"Sounds like I'll be a material witness."

"Sounds that way, Jimmy."

"Pretty serious between you?"

"Serious enough." Mike's crooked smile earned him a chuckle from his foreman. "She has to have someone to help her walk in those shoes."

Jimmy slapped his hand on his manager's shoulder followed with a good laugh. "That much I know. But have yuh spoken to my sister?"

"I will." Mike gripped Jimmy's shoulder for a moment and walked back to his office. Jakki was standing in the corner, looking over her shoulder through the grimy windows. She glanced in his direction, folding her arms across her chest.

"This day started out kind of normal," Mike said, sitting at his desk to face her. "Doesn't usually last long though."

"He offered me a lift."

"You know him?"

"He lives in that house. A friend of Gavin's. He wanted to say he felt bad, then he drove here. I don't know why."

"Odd way of showing he felt bad."

"I thought he was offering me a lift to the theater."

"There's plenty of time."

She wore shorts and fuzzy hiking boots with white fur all around her ankles, a fur beret with some kind of long green feather curling around her chin. *Where does she get this stuff?* Her blouse was tailored and demur except it had no buttons and showed her hot pink lace camisole. *A guy doesn't have a chance.* "Coffee, darlin'?"

"Do you have that flavored creamer?"

"Hazelnut or Vanilla?"

"Either." She slid into the chair in front of his desk and held out her hand.

Something had changed but Mike picked up no specific signals. Just a general sense that she was different. Nothing physical. Hair. Outfit. Shoes. Nothing unusual, at least, not for her. He brought the coffee, to the rim with hazelnut creamer—his favorite if he was in the mood to adulterate a cup of instant that wasn't worth boiling water for—and Jakki clamped her fist around it. Not the slightest tremor. He sat on the desk in front of her, stretched his legs to either side of her chair.

"Ever wonder where these guys come from?"

"Every day."

His laugh filled the Portacabin.

"I find them easily."

"I noticed."

"Or they find me. They've been finding me all my life."

The whole and nothing but the truth hadn't been zapped out of her. Whether her parents messed her up to protect or punish, they failed on all counts. No guy looked at Jakki Hunter without hankering.

"Can't say I blame them, sweetheart."

"They're out of luck." She set the empty cup on his desk and stood, wiggling to straighten her blouse. "This Saturday is the end of the Festival."

twenty-one

Her abrupt announcement took him from mirth to astonished so fast the choke chain snapped. *It's over. Five days and she'll be gone.* "That soon?"

"There's a party and prizes."

He nodded, didn't trust his bark.

"Will you take me?"

"Sure."

"It will be pretty fancy but you'll clean up just fine."

"How high are your shoes going to be?"

"Wait 'til you see."

He smirked at the front of a good chuckle. "Right. Now, I've got to get back to work. Looks like we won't finish this project before October." *She'll be gone before then.* "I'm not looking forward to another winter here." Scottish weather was the least of the misery her declaration promised.

When she insinuated her body between his legs, he looked into her eyes, unable to read any signal she was giving. *It's over. Damn.* He should have seen this coming. Actress, playwright, dancer, looney dame he'd fallen for like a boulder to the bottom of the canyon. Miss her like crazy. Never sleep again, not for long, anyway. She locked her fingers in his hair, looked like she wanted something. His thoughts kept revolving around prone positions, but he kept his hands flat on the desk and met her stare for stare.

"Then you'd better get to work, Mr. Argent." She backed off, shooing him out of his office like a naughty schoolboy.

No one on his crew took notice of him as he slumped back to the routine of his day, heart about to burst with the uselessness of his life when a cab stopped at the gate and his girl slid into the back without a glance.

See it through. What else was there for him? At lunch time, he crawled back into his office. Every paper and file on his desk was in order, each stack with a sticky note on top: identified and coded. He added Administrator to Jakki Hunter's list of accomplishments before he gave thought to his role as her escort at the closing event.

Before he could get to that, his office phone rang and the handheld receiver in his pocket annoyed him. "Yeah?"

"You know what we were talking about this morning?"

"I remember but—."

"Stow it, Mike. The jerk's lawyer just served head office with a restraining order. You can't go near that woman."

"I told you there's nothing to concern the company." He planted his big hand on one stack of documents, marked 'Invoices' in the stylish handwriting of a prep school girl. *Add that to the list.*

Soon he'd have all the reasons why they weren't a fit. Not even close.

"Doesn't matter, Mike. Go anywhere near that woman and you'll lose your job."

"Look, he's just trying it on. And no one, not even the company, has any right to tell me who I can see. You weren't here and you did not see what happened to Miss Hunter. You weren't here this morning to see one of the jerk's henchmen try the same trick. This jerk is the problem, not Jakki. Not me. Either get on my side or butt out."

"Finished?"

Mike held his outrage in check, counted backwards from a thousand. That's how long he figured he'd need to bring his fury under control if Pete Ferguson said another word about his private business.

"What you do on your own time—strictly speaking—is your business, Argent. No one will argue with that. *But.* This is a legal mess. One the management wants contained. This woman is…well, let's just say she's no stranger to lawsuits. Until this is resolved, head office is asking you to back off. The solicitor has sent a restraining order to the woman as well. She won't be allowed on the site until this is sorted, Mike."

"I can live with that. But nothing else. Got it?"

"It's your funeral. Just keep her away from company property."

"Right." He tapped through his contacts and found Mary McEwan's number.

"I've been wondering what it would take to make you see the light," Jimmy's sister said when he'd related the latest developments. "I'll see you in my office in twenty minutes. No excuses."

Armed with all the cautions, rights and permissions his barracuda drilled into his skull, Mike rode over to the quasi-theater. His girl danced across the floor and into his arms, led him on a wild two-step, foxtrot ride. He went along. Her fellow actors and crew members stared as though all they had ever known about her crazy ways was coming true.

"I've been invited to take *Bondage* to Sweden," she whispered, still dancing, pressing her chin on his shoulder, staring into his eyes when he turned his face toward her. He counted the tiny lines on her lower lip that disappeared when she pouted and multiplied when she puckered up. He loved both. Losing both. Dragged a football field length of highway on the bumper of a drunk driver's car didn't hurt as much as this.

"When do you leave?"

"Terrence is organizing everything for me."

If she had offered him a samurai sword, the gut slicing would not have been any more successful. As much as coming to terms with the way it was with her had made him, if not resigned, at least accepting, the reality was a whole other pain.

"How long?" Two words. He choked on both.

"There'll be all the auditions, rehearsals, confirmations, marketing, publicity—."

"How long?"

"The tour starts in April. That's for two months, all over the country."

Mike did the math. "Eight months. And some."

Jakki pressed her chin harder into his shoulder joint.

"Who's going to help you walk in those shoes? Terrence? Yeah?"

"Kevin's tenure with the production ends with the award party. We'll be recruiting a whole new cast."

"Who then?"

A 'kicking' was not strong enough to describe the wreckage in his gut. When she pressed her hands on either side of his jaw, he caught her wrists, as if he could release the tension on the chain. Jakki pouted. Smooth lower lip, plump, killing him. Cast and crew walked by, still looking at them with smirks on their faces. Mike forced a big grin. No way was he letting these jokers know he was losing it.

"That's great, darlin'. You'll kill 'em." A bear hug was as big a relief to him as to her. She wrapped her arms around his neck and danced in his arms, flaunting her good spirits, her happiness.

Deny her that? Not likely, not when he knew the whole story of how she'd fought to get to this moment. "When did you find out? Who invited you?" Was his tone right? Must have been. She didn't stop dancing.

"I can't believe it, Mike. Nothing like this has ever happened to me. Something so incredible. This director from a Swedish arts council. She loves my work. It's a commission, Mike. *A commission*. I'm so excited."

"Your shoes?" She'd need someone. "Tell me it's not Gavin."

"Mike, how could you even think that?" She grinned, slapped his shoulder. "You're a nut."

He didn't confess.

"I'm not that crazy." She pulled back, lifted her gaze to the dingy ceiling. "You think I am."

"I didn't say that." She took a deep breath. He released his hold. "Darlin', it's going to take me a while to get used to—." *Stop right there. It's not about you.* "I'm happy for you, darlin'. Doesn't make it any easier but—."

"This can't be love."

"What is it then?" Just like all the other guys she'd known. Angry she didn't love him, never mind that she couldn't.

"The words to that song. They make sense to me now." She stroked his upper arm for a moment, met his stare with a weak smile. "All my life, I've been scared. Scared I wasn't what I should be. Scared to be crazy. Scared *not* to be crazy because, if I wasn't, something was really wrong." She took his hands and rubbed her cheek over his knuckles. "I feel okay. It's hard but I'm happy. I'm okay."

"Good." What else could he say? "That's good, darlin'." He'd get over it. He'd get through tomorrow and the next day and Monday and the next eight months. He'd get his life back. *Such as it was. Move on.*

"It is. It really is." She exhaled and wrapped her arms around his waist. "I'm hungry. Are you? Can we go to that burger joint again?"

"Sure." All he needed was a stick. Beat himself with it and chase it at the same time. No need now for Jimmy's barracuda sibling.

twenty-two

See it through. He had just three days to convince her to stay. *Some chance.* Beautiful, talented, accomplished, sophisticated, classy. *Yeah, right.* Staying with him, a beat up navvy with nothing but a motorcycle and a decent flat with a good view. What would a girl like her do? *Run, screaming.*

At the end of the day, he rode home in heavy, slick traffic, slipping between cars, pedestrians and buses, controlling the skids and not thinking anymore about what was out of his hands. After he cleaned up, he suited up in his waterproofs and rode back to catch the performance, sitting in the back, nursing a pint of bitter.

Jakki didn't seem surprised he was still hanging around. She walked toward the table and stopped a few feet away. The audience was gone, heading for shelter between downpours. Her producer-partner, or whatever Terrence was, stood a foot to the side, staring at Mike as though he'd committed a crime. Mike tossed the dregs of the bitter down his throat and got to his feet. Not much of a back problem, a twinge, nothing to cry about.

"Hungry, darlin'?"

"Are you trying to get her deported or something?"

Mike didn't even turn his head. He slid a few pound coins on the table for the waitress/usherette and offered his hand to Jakki.

"I can't, Mike."

One step brought him up close. He slid his hands down her arms and stared into her eyes. "Can't or won't?"

"I'm not allowed."

"There's no rule says a woman can't go home."

"But there's a restraining order."

"No judge can make you homeless, even in this country." He laid his hand on her hip and guided her out. The bike was dripping but he helped her into the waterproofs and onto the bike before he saluted at Terrence and rode away, her arms tight around his belly.

"This is all wrong." Jakki dropped her bag and coat on the arm of the sofa, turned on him and folded her arms. "You know I can't stay here. You're not supposed to talk to me."

"Is that what you want? Handy excuse to get out of a mess, right?"

"For you, yes."

"Who's cooking tonight?"

"Don't you care?"

"Okay, I'll cook." He peeled off his leather jacket and rubbed a towel over his head, washed his hands and opened the fridge. "Not a lot of choice, darlin'. Omelet okay?" He pulled cheese and eggs from the door, a selection of vegetables and milk, lined everything up in order of mixing and studied the combination. Satisfied with his choices, Mike turned on the radio, tied a white apron around his middle and started his work.

"Mike."

He glanced at her, acknowledged the problem with a shrug and sliced onion rings.

"This isn't right."

"No, it's not. But I'm not letting anyone tell me I can't have a life because some rich kid can't control his temper."

Jakki sat cross-legged in the doorway. "That's not the whole of it."

"It's what I saw." He whisked the smidgen of milk in the eggs. "And Jimmy."

"That's what it looked like, but that's not all. Be reasonable."

"I don't have to be reasonable. I was an observer. And, strictly interpreting part of the injunction, *we* can't discuss this." Mike cut a pat of butter, melted it in the pan and tested its temperature with a flick of water before he poured the egg mixture and used a spatula to pull the omelet into folds until it was cooked. He added vegetables and cheese, cut it in half and slid them onto warm plates. "Too late for a salad. We'll have desert instead." He stepped over her, set the plates on the coffee table.

Jakki brought knives, napkins and forks. They ate in silence. Mike took long swigs of his bottled beer, sank back and pulled her into his arms.

"I don't know what he's trying to prove or what the whole story is. I don't want or need to know. If you need to tell me, go right ahead but it won't change how much I love you."

Still. Immobile. Frozen. Mike rested his chin on the top of her head. There wasn't much else he could do after he'd dropped that chunk of lead on her. *Again.* There wasn't much she could do either. Take it in. Think it over. Deal with it. *Again. It* being love. *Love. Of all things.* He focused on the misty lights of the street lamps. Where did he get the idea he loved her? He did but that wasn't what she needed to hear. Staying with him? *Why would she ever even think about that?*

Okay, so she turned into him, slid her arms around his chest like she wanted to be with him, but stay? Not in a million heartbeats.

"Yeah well, now you know. No one gets to tell me what I can think or feel. Or what I can have or want to have. My ex made that my Number One 'no'. I love you. Period. No big deal. I'm not asking for anything. No expectations, okay? Do what you want."

They sat. He looked out the big window. Every time he looked down, her eyes were closed, blue, maybe green, eye shadow, silvery black mascara. His back didn't hurt. All the while, he was thinking. *This could work. This is simple. Maybe we'd be okay.*

"I've never been to Sweden."

"Me either." *That's it, the end of the road. She's leaving.* "First, we've got this wrap party."

"That's right." She snuggled harder under his arm. "Would you ever introduce me to your parents?"

"In one, hot micro-second. Say the word and I'll fly them over." Sweden. Meet his parents? *Go figure.* Some things were best taken as they were. Something swelled in his chest, call it possibility. Even hope. *Don't lose your cool. Sleep on it.*

Another day of early start, facing down his smirking crew, giving Ferguson as little aggravation or fuel to fire him as possible but that didn't mean he came even close to succeeding. Not twenty minutes passed before he got the next blow to the midsection.

"I've heard from your solicitor, Argent. Thanks for the warning, by the way. That went over well in the bosses' office."

"Not my call, Pete. Sorry."

"Are you? Sorry? You will be. Once this job's done, you can walk."

"I was planning on it."

"You're a bloody moron. For what?"

Mike held back all the reasons. "What exactly did Ms. McEwan offer?"

"Like you don't know," Ferguson growled, thumping the receiver on his desk. "She's put a restraining order on Gregory and Bassett, that's all. And she's sent the sheriff's bailiffs after your girlfriend's so called assailant, impounded his car or something crazy. And the corker is, your barracuda has filed some *habeas corpus* bull on *his* solicitor."

"That all?" Mike grinned at Jimmy like a fool. His foreman folded his arms, grinning back, obvious pride in his younger sibling all over his face, nodded his head, winked and walked out of the Portacabin before he busted a gut laughing.

"No. You damn well know the company has been put on warning that any communication with your girlfriend without her 'legal representative' present will be a matter for a lawsuit. Where do you get off threatening your employer, Argent? Gregory and Bassett have been good to you. All these years."

"It's just a precaution, to protect Miss Hunter. She's pretty shaken up and gets enough harassment from the jerk and his mouthpiece. That's all."

"All? There's more," Pete hissed. "Where did you find this witch?"

"Personal recommendation, Pete. A friend of mine thought I might need some legal help."

"Listen you, if we weren't behind schedule and you weren't the only site manager within five thousand miles who could pull this project out of the grave, I'd be over there so fast to kick you into England, you'd land in Dover before you took your next breath."

"That's sweet talk, Pete," Mike chuckled. "Glad to know I'm appreciated. Now, is it okay with you if I get back to my job?"

"Does your crew know we've scheduled the continuous pour for Saturday?"

"They know and we'll be ready."

"Damn well better be."

Two more days of work and waiting. Two more nights of sleeping on the sofa—sitting with his arms around her until he fell asleep. *Crazy.*

She got loose Saturday, sometime before dawn, extricated herself, showered and made his breakfast wearing his boot socks and t-shirt. All he could do was stand in the shower until the ache went away, died a miserable, lonely death. *What am I doing? No idea. Not a clue.* Even clunking his head on the shower tiles didn't bring clarity.

"I booked a car and driver for us. For tonight."

"What time, darlin'?"

"Nine. I don't want to be there too early. Terrence and Rache will be taking the table and some of the rest in the cast. The awards don't start until ten so we'll have time to settle."

Probably the longest she'd spoken in two days. He nodded.

"I've rented you a tuxedo too. Terrence hired a kilt and all that but I didn't think you'd want anything that fancy."

He nodded.

"If you're home by six, we'll have time to eat at that Thai place you like."

He nodded. Anytime soon she'd ask him to speak, to think. He wasn't ready for that.

"I'll book ahead just in case we can do that, otherwise we'll have dinner here. I won't eat at the awards, but you can."

He nodded, felt like the choke chain was falling off and that felt worse than hanging by it on the junk yard gate.

"I won't be late." All he could manage before he scooped up his gear and made it out the door without doing something shameful like crying or begging or falling to his knees.

twenty-three

No worse day for feeling like walking straight off the Forth Bridge and come what may after that.

Continuous pour concrete didn't allow for guys with heartache to take a breather so his crew didn't catch on to the red-rimmed eyes. He got through that okay, pretending the cement dust got in his eyes, pretending he was choked up with it.

The pour took seven solid non-stop hours and not one of the crew balked at missing his tea break or lunch or afternoon pint. Made a big change from his crew in that Hammersmith fandango when the Limeys put the mid-morning tea break before doing a proper job. Fortune smiled on him that day—he was only the assistant, not the manager who let it happen. If he had had to stand over this crew with a whip, he'd never have made it, not today, knowing his girl was packing up her life, leaving him behind.

Another slip of his grip like that and he'd be throwing himself in the cement and be glad to be buried. Hell of a thing to be in love with a quirky girl with more brains than he could muster. *Shoot me now.*

"Jimmy, you got this?"

"Sure do, Mike. We're toppin' off now."

Mike stepped back from his vigil, watched the truck crank down and shimmy to a stop. Two of his guys whipped the flywheels around and shut off the flow. No air trapped. No dead bodies. Not even a site manager floating on the surface.

"Good job." He owed them more than that. He pushed his hardhat back, clamped his hand on Jimmy's shoulder, saluted the eight-man crew who'd stuck it out through a grueling day. "Heroic, gentlemen. Great work. First round's on me, but not tonight. Let's cap and get out."

"You got it, boss."

A couple of the crew cheered. A few leaned on girders and lit up. Mike shoved his hands in his pockets and hung his head.

On his way back through the streets, he left off thinking about tomorrow. His job for the night was clear.

His apartment was empty.

Mike took his time getting clean and into the tux. Perfect fit. He braved a look at the mirror. *Okay. Not embarrassing.* Passed for smart anyway. Shoes so shiny they caught the lights from the street and sparkled. A big car rolled toward the building. Jakki waved from the backseat.

He took his key and walked down the stairwell. Blocked everything that crowded into his head until he sat beside her. Why did she have to be everything he wanted?

"You look nice."

"You're the most beautiful woman I've ever known."

"Thank you." This time, the shoes were well beyond crazy. No way was she going to walk in them without help. One skinny strap over her toes and a thick collar around her ankles. Heels like needles.

"Where do you find these shoes?"

"I have connections." She moved closer to him, leaned in. "Have you ever been to an awards party?"

The dress was a skimpy sheath of black silk, shiny and slick, floating around her thighs like a summer storm about to bust loose with lightning and thunder. Quickening his blood, stirring his soul, energizing his spirit. Still, there was something missing. He patted the inside pocket of his tuxedo jacket.

"Not to speak of. Closest thing was a construction industry 'Crew of the Year' commendation."

"You'll be fine," Jakki laughed, wrapping her arm around his. "I've never done anything like this. I'm glad you're experienced."

The limo pulled in behind another fancy car in a line of fancy cars but it was a show without an audience. The entrance to the hotel was clear except for a television camera truck and a reporter doing her best to pretend she wasn't the only reporter on the scene. The wind and fog had made *their* grand red carpet entrance to steal the limelight from the artists and performers. Fringe folks dashed into the hotel, shoving past the reporter and cameraman to get to shelter.

Mike went around the back of the car just as the driver opened the door and Jakki's left foot appeared. If he hadn't known what was farther up that would have been enough for him to fall in love. The cameraman must have felt the same, making a bee-line for the limo with his camera running and the reporter in pursuit.

Mike beat his rival to offer his hand to help Jakki out and to steady her when she got there. The reporter's mic was in her face before she knew who held it. Her recoil was intense, caught on camera, but Mike resisted his instinct to push the handheld microphone back into the reporter's face.

He got in the way until Jakki understood what was happening and took control of the situation. True to her quirks, she took the mic in both hands and said, "This evening isn't about winning or losing in any creative endeavor. The popularity of your work is immaterial. Integrity counts. Creation counts. Generosity counts. If I have accomplished any of these, I will have done my job."

"Thank you, Miss Hunter. And good luck." The reporter turned to the cameraman, forcing him to take his lens off Mike's date. "And that was Jakki Hunter, author and performer in one of the *many* experimental productions."

144

The emphasis the reporter put on "many" annoyed Mike but he let it go. He offered his arm and, after a noticeable hesitation, Jakki took it.

The reporter smiled at him. Not the kind of smile a reporter gives to the underling of an interviewee. Not the kind of smile a construction engineer who'd just pulled a seven-hour continuous pour shift ever got. This kind of smile was the kind of smile a guy gets from a girl who thinks she'd like to know him.

Mike smiled back. Not the kind of smile a guy gives a girl he wants to know. This smile said, *Sorry, spoken for*.

Jakki pressed her temple against his jaw and he stole a quick kiss. *This could work. Maybe.* Still hopeful. Beyond help or redemption. In the last throes of total capitulation.

She was less stable on the way up the two steps to the hotel foyer but no one noticed. His arm was that much steadier to make sure her entrance was sublime.

The table reserved for the *Bondage* crew was center middle, perfect if it weren't for the serving station beside them.

Jakki took a seat facing the front of the dining hall. Mike took the seat to her left, closest to the station. Terrence and Rache were already there. Neither seemed to have any interest in seeing the stage, concentrating all their energies on who was nearby and who they might next accost.

Mike was unperturbed by the repeated shuffling of his chair to make room for one or another of Jakki's fellow Fringers. She deserved that much attention and stood to accept all incoming hugs and kisses. He ignored the fawning and cooing, made eye contact with the waiter. With the promise of being served, he relaxed back in his chair as much as his dodgy spine allowed.

He admired his date's ability to maintain her balance, even under extreme conditions of flailing arms, as men and women wrapped her up with caresses and heavy perfumes.

By nine:thirty, the rest of the cast and crew had arrived and Mike had been shunted around so his back was to the stage and the *Bondage* waitress/usherette was next to him. She gave him a tentative smile. He winked in return which she received with more satisfaction than he'd meant. His eyes were fixed on Jakki, directly opposite him, a roundtable seating of twelve away and adrift.

When the waiter set a glass in front of him, Mike didn't care what was in it. He drank fast and deep. Jakki looked like he felt—out of place and ready to run.

He finished the whiskey and left the table. Before he skirted the flow of waiters and late arrivals, Jakki's expression registered distress and hopeless acceptance. He couldn't get near her fast enough.

The ceremony began with fanfare and what felt like a hundred pipers, all crushing down on the overcrowded room.

"Take my seat," he murmured. Yeah looked up at him, attempted a smirk, threatened refusal, capitulated when Mike shifted the actor's chair back. "Please?" Although Mike choked on the civility, Yeah grumbled and surrendered to brute force in a tuxedo, no less threatening for shiny lapels.

"Didn't know you hired him as a heavy, Jak."

Jakki stared in her most vacant way at her fellow cast member and made no effort to confirm or refute Yeah's comment. Mike didn't care either way. His job was self-determined and he intended to be damned good for any and all scenarios.

"Do you want a drink, darlin'?"

"Just water."

Mike held up his hand to the next culinary service provider passing the table and ordered his preferences. Others at the table chimed in.

"What's the deal?" he asked the waiter.

"However you wish to pay, sir."

"I'll foot the bill for me and this lady."

"As you wish," the waiter replied and moved on.

Jakki voiced no objections but when the drinks came in batches and her cast members were digging for cash, she turned to Mike. He closed his fingers over her hand and shook his head. He leaned close and murmured, "You don't owe anyone anything, darlin'.""

She nodded and curled her fingers around the glass of ice water the waiter set in front of her. Mike touched his glass to hers and took a swallow of the single malt straight up, nodded his approval of the quality and turned his attention to the stage.

He flinched when someone grabbed his shoulders and shook him. From the aggression of the act, Mike had no doubt who stood behind him. One glance at Jakki confirmed it. In one move, he shoved his chair back and dislodged Gavin Andrews's hold on him.

"Hey, hey," the roadster jerk complained, raising his hands. "Just saying hello, laddie."

Mike stood and faced his adversary, took a deep breath, recalling all the cautionary directions he had from Ms. Mary McEwan. "I'm not surprised to see you here, but if you attempt to circumvent the terms of the injunction, I will see you in court."

"Considering what you threatened before, Mickey-lad, you've gone soft." The jerk tipped his hand to Jakki and grabbed a chair from another table, pushing it between Terrence and Rache, facing Jakki and forcing them to move back to accommodate him. Gavin laid his arm on the back of Rache's chair, leaned close and whispered in her ear, blowing into the front of her low-cut dress.

Mike patted his date's knee and said, "He can't touch you, speak to you, or harass you in anyway."

"Why?"

Surefire trouble. She didn't see the world the way he did. She took the blame for everything that happened to her and, in a way, she was right. But Gavin Andrews was responsible for his actions too and Mike's job was to help Jakki Hunter walk in the shoes she chose to wear.

"Because you need someone on your side."

She cocked her head to the side, considering for a moment, before she nodded her acquiescence to his explanation. "I don't need to talk to him, anyway. He's not backing the tour in Sweden."

So typical of his girl to avoid any confrontation, pretending the jerk's appearance had no importance, nothing to do with her, nothing to be concerned about. If Mike didn't know better, he'd believe she had no care in the world.

"Good to know," he answered, despite the reminder that he had only a few days left to convince her he should be part of her life. "Now all you need is someone to help you walk in those shoes." He smiled and tipped his glass to her. "Take a walk with me, darlin'?"

twenty-four

The lobby was a mausoleum by comparison. Jakki leaned on his arm, followed to the foyer and out into the crisp night. The street was wet. The television reporter and cameraman were gone. The marquee awning offered shelter from the rain but none from the blasts of North Sea gales.

"Do you want to stay, Jakki?"

She looked up at the drizzle falling through the swathe of street lights. "We have the car until two AM."

Not an answer to his question, an alternative. "I don't want to take you away from your friends or spoil your evening but if this guy—."

"I'm okay if you want to go."

"I'm not leaving you. Not while Andrews is around to spew his venom. You shouldn't have to endure that."

"You want to go."

"What I want is irrelevant. Tonight is about you. What do *you* want?" Wrong to push but the time had come. Her choice. He knew his.

Sudden tears. A vacant stare. Thought and confusion. "I want to stay."

Something. A clear choice. One push more. "Do you want me to stay with you?"

Eyes clenched. Expression perplexed. Searching inside, no distractions or looking for the answer anywhere else, not looking to him to know the correct answer.

"Yes. Yes, I want you to stay here with me until the end of the ceremony."

"Why?" Unfair, torture, pulling the wound open. Not doing himself any favors. He had to know.

This time with eyes open. A step forward, hands on his lapels, soothing, supplicant. The choke chain could never get any tighter. He stopped trying to breathe.

"Because I'm scared. I don't want to be scared." She shivered like a puppy, slipping into his embrace, "I don't want them to know how scared I am."

Mike tightened his arms, hugged her tight. "There's only one way, darlin'. You've been protecting yourself pretty well most of your life. Now it's my turn. And it will be my pleasure, Miss Hunter."

"This is wrong. I don't know what to do. Is it wrong, Mike? Is this how it feels?"

"How what feels, darlin'?"

"Love. It can't be love. How do you feel, Mike?"

"Scared."

"Really? Is that love?"

"It must be. I'm scared all the time. But I know I love you."

His girl hadn't yet bought the declaration. No matter how often he told her, the barrier of her experience rose between them, like the cold stones of the houses surrounding the Princes Street park.

"Why are you scared?"

She hung him on the chain link fence and demanded he come clean, turn belly up and let her flail him alive. Although she didn't know she was doing it, his courage for that truth faltered. Mike eased the silk tie around his neck, cleared his throat. Looking everywhere but into her eyes, he laughed and shook his head. "Darlin', this is love. It's scary to put my heart and my future in your hands, not just any hands, *your* hands, Jakki. And not because of anything you've done," he assured her, quick to read her guilt mechanism in play. "For me, you're perfect but we're different, maybe we want different things, but

I want you in my life. If that's not possible, it's a good reason to be scared, right?"

Nothing. The closest she came to a response was to cock her head to the side, puzzlement the closest description he could find for her expression. Maybe she was mulling his speech over. Maybe in shock or disbelief. Maybe in complete ignorance. Twisting away from him, she clasped his hand and strode, as best she could on her needle-heels, back to the banquet room. Mike kept up, stayed behind, figuring she didn't intend to dump him that night.

Their chairs were still empty, pushed closer together to fit more cast and crew around the table. Jakki eased into the narrow space. Mike dropped into his chair, filled her water glass and kissed her cheek. Yeah smirked. Waitress/Usherette clapped the tips of her fingers together in glee. Gavin's stare hardened as two of his Citizen Henchmen approached the table.

The emcee was a familiar face in the Fringe festivities to most of the audience but Mike couldn't place him, except as a self-important blackguard with a filthy mouth. The audience loved him. The more often he used primitive Anglo-Saxon, the more they guffawed and applauded.

The lesser awards came first. The category *Bondage* had been nominated for was scheduled for the second half of the evening. More than a little irritated, Mike shifted in his chair to readjust his spine. Jakki neither smiled nor laughed.

"And this," the emcee concluded the first half of the awards segment, "has just been announced. Four of the experimental productions have won grants to perform—I know what you're thinking..." he paused to make a gesture that allowed no other interpretation of the word *perform*, "—abroad."

The audience howled with appreciation.

"*Flipped, Forestalled, Whatever He Said* and *Bondage,* of all things, will be touring in Scandinavia and the EU next year."

The cast and crew around the table leapt to their feet cheering. Three other tables erupted at the same time. The applause for the four productions was polite from other Fringe participants.

"Don't let it go to your head," Gavin sneered at Terrence. "The laddies over there don't care what they see as long as they get something from the Fringe." His henchmen laughed and nodded, filth pouring out of their mouths as they made crude gestures. "That Swedish lass bought this show for the title. Once she gets a look at the script, she'll realize the only good thing about it is the title. I'm laughing," he claimed, slapping his pocket, "and so is my bank account."

His henchmen guffawed, rolled their eyes and slapped their First Citizen on the shoulder. The ruckus they made when they laughed and pointed at Jakki attracted the attention of the emcee.

"That's right," he slurred, rolling his hips and throttling the mic. "That's Jakki Hunter. The *Bondage* Queen. We all know what that means."

Gavin leaned back in his chair, gave the emcee a thumbs up. Several more of his henchmen circled the table, pointing and howling like lunatics, chanting, "We know what that means. We know what that means."

"I think you need this tonight." Mike slipped his fingers into his inside pocket and plucked out the hideous green bow he'd saved from the rain puddle nights before.

"I thought I lost this," Jakki gasped. "Where did you find it?"

"I rescued it a while ago. I meant to give it back sooner but tonight seems like the right occasion."

"I love this bow," she sighed, holding it against her heart. "I thought Gavin threw it away, or one of the others, when he threw me out of the house." She wrapped the ribbon cock-eyed around her head and set the bow just above her temple. Mike nodded his approval, kissed the opposite temple and offered his hand. She squeezed his arm against her breasts. "Thank you, Mike."

The laughter in the ballroom reached a pitch that rivalled the emcee's raunchy tributes to the local VIPs and the humiliation of the four productions, threatening to drown out even the pipers who closed the first half of the evening. With no distracting competition for his sideshow, Gavin Andrews pushed his chair back, rose and called attention to his mob, jived them up with a salute of his glass of blended malt on ice.

Mike glanced at his straight up single malt, decided against taking a swig and reached for his cell.

"Who are you calling?"

"My barracuda," he murmured.

Jakki covered his phone with her hand and shook her head. "Don't. That will only make it worse."

"You don't have to put up with this, darlin'. Let me get my crew out here. We'll take care of these cowards in two seconds."

His girl shook her head, true to her quirks, prepared to take the blame, accept her guilt for their angry resentment of her success. "Will you kiss me, Mike?"

He slid his chair back, knocking a hole in the circling mob, as he steadied Jakki and wrapped her up in an extravagant embrace—her declared, acknowledged lover. His nymph slid her arms around her heavy's neck, stared the whining dog down and called out the wolf. No pipes, no chanting, no snide remarks, relentless as they were, broke the spell.

"And I won't need anyone in Sweden to help me walk in my shoes, Mike," his girl whispered. "I'm leaving all my crazy shoes here, but I'll wear them when I meet your parents."

This is how it was. He'd never change the way the dust settled in the end, wasn't sure he'd want to. It suited him just fine but it could have gone either way. One event, one day, one need, one desire at a time. The rest, the future, the next challenge— uncharted, undiscovered, unknown and nothing he could or wanted to do anything about.

Yeah could smirk all he damn well pleased. Gavin and his Citizen Henchmen could play all the tricks in their slimy books. None of them had what it took to bring down lovers who'd won—over all the odds and evens in any gambler's hand.

Jakki swayed in his arms. Mike clasped her hand and, with no clue what he was doing, two-stepped beyond the mob, into the path of the service staff, dancing to the drone of the blasted pipes and the beat of her heart against his.

"Will you catch me if I stumble?" she whispered against his lips.

"Count on it, darlin'."

Pete Ferguson would be all over him on Monday for involving Jimmy but, he'd left his call to Mary McEwan open. When two uniformed policemen badged their way through the tables, Mike chuckled.

"This should be good."

Jakki met the promise with a glance, then a wide-eyed stare in Gavin's direction. "What are they doing? Where are they taking him?"

"To jail, I hope. My lawyer, who also happens to be Jimmy's sister, is married to a cop who is Jimmy's best friend. This works for me," Mike replied.

Whatever came of the arrest, Jakki made no objection, took no blame to counter the outcome. While the circling henchmen dispersed without a second glance at their pack leader, his nymph glided into her chair, reached for a bottle and poured champagne into her own glass.

He'd promised his crew a round of drinks. If he still worked for Gregory and Bassett after this, he'd step up for more than a round until he took the first job they offered anywhere near his girl, even if that meant going home.

after words

Thank you for reading **This Can't Be Love**, the latest Big City Romance novel in my **Americans in Love** series, set in cities around the world. Previous in this series is my debut novel, *Wait a Lonely Lifetime*, set in Florence, featured on the Florence Tourist Office's website. Forthcoming novels in the series include *Dance by the Light of the Moon*, set in Wales, Chicago and Arizona:

Dance by the Light of the Moon

Marshall Gregory, a washed-up running-back, still runs from the injury that put him on the bench and into the world of international corporate team-building.

Colette Ilar, acting branch manager of a regional bank, doesn't believe in teamwork, especially not the kind that brings unwanted attention and gets her nowhere fast.

He's not looking for a future. She's not looking for the love of her life.

If you've enjoyed reading this book, other Big City Romances you may also enjoy are *Salsa Dancing with Pterodactyls*, set in San Francisco, and my serial novel, *Nights Before*, set in Portland, Maine.

My forthcoming historical novel, *Pavane for Miss Marcher*, is set in Maine.

Pavane for Miss Marcher

Giggling girls grow up, sometimes when they least expect and in unexpected ways. Events and experience follow Cathryn Marcher from her hometown in Maine to the makeshift war hospital in Boston and back again.

Rupert Smith enlisted in the Union Army for all the reasons his upbringing demanded of him. When events and experience threaten to destroy him, the giggling girl he remembers is his only link to the man he may never be again.

Other Books by Leigh Verrill-Rhys

Anthologies (Editor)

On My Life, 1987
Parachutes & Petticoats, 1992, 2002, 2010
Iancs, Conshîs, a Spam, 2002

Author of:

Wait a Lonely Lifetime, 2012

The serial novel, *Nights Before:*
Nights Before: #1, 'Twas the Night Before New Year, 2012
Nights Before: #2, 'Twas the Night Before Valentine's Day, 2013
Nights Before: #3, 'Twas the Night Before Mother's Day, 2013
Nights Before: #4, 'Twas the Night Before Labor Day, 2013
Nights Before: #5, 'Twas the Night Before Veterans Day, 2013
Nights Before: #6, 'Twas the Night Before Christmas Eve, 2013

Salsa Dancing with Pterodactyls, 2014

Forthcoming novels
Dance by the Light of the Moon
Pavane for Miss Marcher

Columnist and Contributor:

Western Mail, 1984-1985
Y Faner, 1981-1984
Discovering Welshness, 1992
Cambria: The Magazine of Wales, 2009

Blogs:

EverWriting, 2009-Present
Avalon Authors, 2010-2013
Ink on the Carpet, 2010-Present
Classic and Cozy Books, 2013-Present

Readers' praise for *Wait a Lonely Lifetime*

"This book is a well-thought out romance novel which shows how life can often come around full circle and complete itself. Fate, destiny, call it what you will, the connection between the two lovers in this book is highly believable. The setting in Florence adds atmosphere and is beautifully described…." — Mrs. Rochester

"*Wait a Lonely Lifetime* was an enjoyable read. It made me want to read other books by this author. I liked her characters." — Barbara Jamile

"Read for 6 solid hours. When I turned the last page I was so disappointed, I wanted the story to go on. I want to know more - how did they handle the Ex's threats, did Eric & Sylviana have a baby, what happened with Enid & Eva? If I'm really lucky, maybe we'll get a sequel." — Martha

"This was a most enjoyable book to read - a romance novel for 'mature' women! Romance can recur. The ex-husband was very credible, unfortunately - gain the 'unattainable goal' then - dump her. Loved the setting in Italy and enjoyed the extended Italian family. Fun reading!" — Mrs. Charles S.

If you would like to share your thoughts about this, or
any of my other books, please comment on
facebook.com/LeighVerrill-RhysAuthor,
twitter.com/EverWriting9, everwriting.wordpress.com,
inkonthecarpet.blogspot.com,
classicandcozybooks.blogspot.com
or visit
leighverrillrhys.com.

All the best,

Leigh Verrill Rhys

♥ ♥ ♥ ♥ ♥